HOOP DREAMS

A PODIUM SPORTS ACADEMY BOOK

LORNA SCHULTZ NICHOLSON

JAMES LORIMER & COMPAN
TORONT(

James Lorimer & Company Ltd., Publishers acknowledges the support of the Ontario Arts Council. We acknowledge the financial support of the Government of Canada through the Canada Book Fund for our publishing activities. We acknowledge the support of the Canada Council for the Arts which last year invested $24.3 million in writing and publishing throughout Canada. We acknowledge the Government of Ontario through the Ontario Media Development Corporation's Ontario Book Initiative.

Cover design: Meredith Bangay
Cover image: Shutterstock

Library and Archives Canada Cataloguing in Publication

Schultz Nicholson, Lorna, author
    Hoop dreams / Lorna Schultz Nicholson.

(Podium Sports Academy)
Issued in print and electronic formats.
ISBN 978-1-4594-0588-2 (bound).--ISBN 978-1-4594-0587-5 (pbk.).--
ISBN 978-1-4594-0589-9 (epub)

    I. Title. II. Series: Schultz Nicholson, Lorna Podium Sports Academy.

PS8637.C58H66 2014   jC813'.6   C2013-906819-8

James Lorimer & Company Ltd.,
Publishers
317 Adelaide Street West, Suite 1002
Toronto, ON, Canada
M5V 1P9
www.lorimer.ca

Distributed in the United States by:
Orca Book Publishers
P.O. Box 468
Custer, WA, USA
98240-0468
Printed and bound in Canada.

Printed and bound in Canada
Manufactured by Friesens Corporation in Altona, Manitoba, Canada in March 2014.
Job #201009

CHAPTER ONE

The applause died down and I sucked in a deep breath. I shook out my legs, tucked in my jersey, and adjusted my purple headband so all my wild Afro hair was slicked off my face. I exhaled. I was next, and the last one on my basketball team to run onto the court like a star for the visiting parents in the stands. This was our second and final Parents Weekend. To me this was over-the-top Hollywood stuff.

Most parents loved it, though.

Don't cry. Don't cry.

The instructions were to wait on the other side of the door leading to the gym until your name was called. Then you were to take a red rose from the volunteer standing at the door, run in, and hand it to your mother, who would be lined up with the other mothers at mid-court.

Why did *my* team have to be playing tonight — Opening Night? Every other player on my team thought we were the lucky ones. They were excited to hand over the rose, and give a hug and a kiss on the cheek to say thanks. Lucky? Yeah right.

As I looked into the gymnasium, I noticed that the

bleachers were crammed with people, every available seat filled. I could feel the buzzing energy from where I stood. My body trembled.

"And captain of Podium's female basketball team," the announcer's voice boomed over the loudspeaker, "Allie McLean!"

I blinked back tears.

A smiling man handed me a rose and I ran onto the court. The crowd roared. I didn't look at anyone, just ran to mid-court, where my best friend, Carrie, was waiting for me. She was my mother's stand-in, a pinch-hitter in baseball terms. I handed Carrie the rose.

She winked at me and mouthed, "Smile."

I faked a big one and waved to the crowd.

I was sure I could hear them murmuring, though. Yeah, it figured, everyone would be wondering where *my* mother was. Only two of us didn't have a mother standing on the mid-court line. But my teammate, Karen Johanson, had a good excuse: her mother had died when she was little. And to top it off, her grandmother had flown in for the event. I was the *only one* without any family present. Most parents saw Parents Weekend as a big deal and they drove or flew in from all over the country to attend. Not mine. Even my billet mom was too busy. Abigail, with her pressed power suits and silk blouses, was out of town on business. I had even begged my mother to send my fifteen-year-old sister, Kat, and she'd just said, "It costs too much."

I wasn't even worth the price of airfare to her.

Don't cry. Don't cry.

Once I'd done my flash to the crowd, I turned back to

Carrie. "Thanks." I almost choked on my word.

"Chin up, buttercup," she whispered back.

I nodded. That was what we said to each other when things were bad. Thankfully, Carrie had come to my rescue. At least I had someone to give the stupid rose to. She'd told me her mother would fill in, but I'd said no. I wanted Carrie.

As a team we waved to the crowd, then moved toward our bench to get ready for the game. I jumped on the spot to warm up. The movement made me feel better. It was time to play ball and that was all that mattered to me. I was going to Duke University next year on a scholarship, and no one there would have to know that my family sucked.

Coach Cathy patted me on the back. "I know that was hard," she said.

I stared her in the eyes. "I'm here to play basketball."

She nodded once and winked at the same time. "I know that."

I pulled an elastic band off my wrist and pulled my hair into a ponytail that looked more like a black wire brush. "Don't feel sorry for me." I held my chin high.

She patted my shoulder. "That's my Allie." She paused. "Knee feeling okay?"

"Yup," I said. "She's fine."

"Keep wearing the brace. It will help."

"For sure," I said. Then I added, "Don't worry, Coach."

She turned her attention to the team. "Okay, girls," she called out, "come on in!" Once the entire team was circled around her, she said, "Remember what we talked about in practice. They have some good shooters. Guards, move your feet. Forwards, find the open space. Allie, rebounds.

Marla, if you can take a three-point shot, take it. And, second string, be ready to go in at any moment."

We stuck our hands in the middle and yelled, "Podium!"

The whistle blew and we ran onto the court. I took my place at centre for the jump ball. At six foot two, I was the tallest on my team and Coach Cathy liked me playing centre. I squatted low and stared at the ball. The ref threw it in the air and I exploded. As soon as I felt the hard rubber on my fingers, I flicked the ball back to Marla Smyth, our best guard. Marla snatched it out of the air, turned, and dribbled as only she could do, under her legs and around her back and away from the opponent. Five foot seven but compactly built, Marla had the quickest reaction time of anyone on our team. And a great vertical jump.

I took off down the court with the rest of my teammates: Lydia, Breanne, and Karen. Karen was another guard and Lydia and Breanne were forwards. The other team was obviously playing a one-on-one system because I was trailed by a blond, ponytailed girl who was not as tall as I was but a lot thicker. Before the game, I'd read all about her. I knew she would be strong on the ball and they'd put her on me for a reason: to stop me from catching rebounds and shooting. And that was okay with me. I'd find a way. My long limbs were my biggest physical asset. They gave me good reach.

Marla successfully brought the ball down the court and I pivoted forward and back and side to side to get away from my shadow. I had to get in the open. Finally I moved sharply one way and my shadow followed, just as I wanted her to. I darted across the court, leaving her behind.

"Open!" I yelled.

Marla sent me a bounce pass. I grabbed the ball and jumped. But instead of shooting for the basket, I passed off to Breanne, who caught the ball and took a shot.

It bounced off the rim, and in two long strides, I jumped to catch the rebound. Before I landed, though, I shot. The ball swirled on the rim twice before sinking through the hoop. When I landed, my knee buckled a little.

Yes! We were on the scoreboard.

"Stay on her!" the coach for the other team called out. Already, I'd rattled them.

I raced downcourt to play defence. Coach Cathy had instructed us to play a zone defence system.

Our opponents were a top team from a high school in Oregon. Last year they had won All State. They moved the ball back and forth with good speed, trying to find an opening. Out of the corner of my eye, I saw Breanne move forward. She was going to intercept!

I broke out and took off down the court.

Breanne snatched the ball mid-air and lobbed it to me. Without breaking stride, I caught it and dribbled as pounding footsteps sounded behind me. I did a layup and sank the ball.

The high tempo of the game continued as we hammered back and forth.

Just before the half, the score was 31–25 for us. We were in their end. Marla had control again and I could see Karen down the side. If Marla could get the ball to me, I could get it to Karen. I eyed Marla, trying to get a read from her.

She dribbled with her left hand, on my side. Time was ticking by. If she didn't hurry, we wouldn't have time to shoot.

We needed to get that one last shot. I dashed forward and she fired a chest pass to me with just seconds on the clock.

The crowd screamed, "Shoot!"

I turned, jumped, and shot.

The ball swished through the hoop and down, just as the buzzer sounded. Three points!

Marla ran over to me. "Great shot."

I high-fived her. "Thanks, girl. Great pass."

"You're on fire tonight," she said.

Yup, I thought. *And there's no one here to watch me.*

Whatever. Who cared? I lifted my chin and looked at Marla. "We all are. Let's take it to 'em second half and really rack up the points."

I grabbed a towel and sat down on the bench, patting my face and chest. My headband was soaked. I fiddled with my brace, making sure it was set to give me the best protection.

"Good execution, ladies," said Coach Cathy. "I think the zone defence is working well. I wouldn't be surprised if they switch to zone next half. If they do, look for the holes. Karen, don't be afraid to hug the line if they push you out. Shoot for three. We can fight for the rebounds." She looked at me. "Allie, be ready to move."

"You betcha," I said.

I glanced around at all my teammates. "We're doing great, guys. Let's keep it up and keep shooting. Let's draw some fouls too." I grinned. "We love doin' that."

"I've been practicing," said Breanne, pretending to box a bit. She was by far the toughest player on our team.

I laughed. "You sure have."

The ref blew his whistle to start the second half. Again,

I took my place at centre and again I won the jump ball. I was probably ninety percent this year on jump balls.

As we headed downcourt, Marla threw the ball to Karen. She dribbled for a few seconds, then tossed the ball to Lydia, who sent it to me. My lane to the basket was clogged, so I sent the ball back to Marla and moved in. Back and forth, all crisp, clean passes. Finally I saw my line. I snatched the ball mid-air and took my two strides. An opposing teammate jumped up with me, trying to push me off the ball. She aggressively knocked me sideways, but I managed to get a shot off before I fell to the floor.

The ref blew his whistle and announced a foul for the other team while I was still on the floor. Lydia ran to me and held out her hand. I grabbed it and stood. No pain. All good.

At the top of the key, I focused on the basket. Practice makes perfect and I practiced my free throws every day. I sank both. The crowd cheered and then we were back on defence.

As predicted, we took it to them in the second half. By the end of the game, I had totalled thirty-five points for my personal best.

Ever.

"Too bad your folks couldn't have been here tonight," said Lydia Kramer as we walked to the dressing room. Lydia came from a small town in northern British Columbia and had been this huge star in her high school. I swear, her parents visited the school every second weekend to watch her play and went to most of our out-of-town games. Unlike my parents, who never came, not together, not separately.

"No biggie." I shrugged.

The elation I felt from accomplishing a personal best came crashing to a halt, and that emptiness I'd felt before the game returned.

"My mother couldn't afford the trip," I mumbled.

Lydia linked her arm with mine. "Hey, my parents are taking me for something to eat. You wanna join us?"

Leave it to freckle-faced Lydia to pick up on my feelings. The girl had this radar that picked up on moods and tried to fix them. Her team nickname was Lovely Lydia. No one ever found fault with her. "Thanks so much for the offer," I replied, "but I've got a date."

A smile that reached to her green eyes spread across her face, and she bumped me with her hip. "You got another guy? You move fast, girl. Who's the lucky one this time?"

"Yeah." Marla butted into the conversation. "Who you hitting on now, Allie-bean?" The "bean" in my nickname was because I was built like a string bean. It was kind of dumb, but everyone on our team had a nickname. Marla's nickname was Mucky Marla because she was always mucking things up on the court, playing games with our opponents.

I playfully smacked Marla on the arm. "Whaddaya mean, *now*? And who says I'm hitting on him? Might be the other way around."

"Yeah, well, you dumped Nathan and Donald. Who's next on your list?" Marla joked.

I laughed. "Jonathon."

Lydia's eyes widened. "He's so hot!"

"All the rowers are hot," said Marla. "I want one too." She jutted out her bottom lip and put her hands on her hips. We all laughed.

"Who's hot?" Breanne had now joined us. Breanne was Bruiser Breanne because she was a bruiser on the court, and liked to jab and elbow when the ref wasn't looking.

"Jonathon," said Marla giggling. "Allie-bean is going for the hottest guy in the entire school."

"Enough!" I held up my hands. We laughed as we walked into the dressing room. I loved my Podium teammates because, although we didn't hang out together all the time, we got along really well, on and off the court. We had the best team spirit with little dramatics.

I flopped down on the bench, took off my high-top runners, and slipped off my brace. Then I placed an ice pack on my knee. After ten minutes, I threw the pack aside and undressed, grabbing my towel to wrap around me.

I stood under the warm water with my head back, letting it soak my hair and cascade down my back. It had been a good night, but it would have been *nice* if my mother had at least *tried* to come. I'd even offered to pay for part of her ticket with *my* savings from last summer. That idea went over like a bomb.

I lowered my head. I hated her for making me feel so lousy. Up, down, up, down. I'd be happy for a bit, then this horrible feeling would wash over me.

Why had I said that about Jonathon? Was that what everyone thought of me? That I just went from one guy to the next? It was true that I'd get close to a guy, then suddenly I'd just shut down, reject the advances, and push him away.

I couldn't hang on to anything in my life except a basketball.

CHAPTER TWO

The crowd of parents and grandparents in the school's front lobby was huge. I stood on tiptoe, which allowed me to see over most of the heads, many of them grey. Where was Jonathon? The guy was six foot four and built like a Greek god so he shouldn't be hard to spot. When I couldn't see him anywhere, my heart sank. Had he ditched me? Fortunately I spotted Carrie way across the room, standing with her mother.

I dodged bodies until I was beside her.

"Awesome game," Carrie said, punching me lightly on the shoulder.

"I'll say," said her mother. "It was like you couldn't miss."

"Thanks," I said to both of them.

"We're going to dinner," said Carrie. "Come with us."

Again, I searched the noisy crowd. When I couldn't see him anywhere, I turned back to Carrie. "I'm supposed to go out with Jonathon."

"He left," said Carrie. "With his folks. Said he had an early morning. I was sure he said he texted you."

"Nooo," I moaned. "My phone's dead." I yanked it out

and tried to turn it on again. But no go. It was toast.

"Shocking," said Carrie sarcastically. "It's from the Dark Ages."

The phone was old, a relic, and the battery barely held a charge anymore.

Carrie put her arm through mine and said, "You need to celebrate after a game like that. Please."

I smiled even though my heart felt as if it weighed more than my new combat boots.

"That's the spirit," said Carrie. Then she looked at her mom. "I'll drive with Allie. Meet you there."

"Sure, honey."

Honey. When was the last time anyone had called me that?

Carrie and I walked to my car without saying anything. I just didn't feel like talking and truth be told, I didn't feel like going to dinner either. But I also didn't want to go home to an empty house. I unlocked my crappy little car and got in. First thing I did was plug in my phone to the car charger.

"You had a great game," said Carrie.

"A personal best." I started my car and it coughed before it fired completely.

"It's not your fault your mom didn't come."

"I hate her."

"Yeah, I don't blame you."

I turned to Carrie. "I'm okay."

"I know. But I get how pissed you are."

"Pissed ain't the word."

"Hey, did you talk to Parm?"

"No, why?"

"Talk about pissed off. She's one mad chick."

"What?" My voice echoed off the front window.

Carrie sniffed her rose, then stuck it behind her ear. "I got the flower."

"You serious?" I shook my head. "Whatever."

"I think she likes you."

"Well, we are friends," I said. "I hope she likes me."

"That's not what I mean, and you know it. And I'm not the only one who thinks so."

Parmita was a good friend of mine and the female soccer team's goalie. She'd recently come out as a lesbian. This, of course, didn't change the way I felt about her. To me, she was a caring, loyal friend. "What's that supposed to mean?"

"One of her soccer confidantes is convinced she's in love with you. It's a rumour going round." She shrugged and winked at me. "Nice to be loved."

I smiled. Carrie had this offbeat sense of humour but always made me laugh. "It's just a rumour," I said. It was true that Parm had this crazy focus that just never shut off — a focus on everything, including academics, sport, and *friendship*. "You're reading way too much into this. She's just intense."

"Order what you want," said Carrie's mother.

I scanned the menu and looked for the cheapest dish. Laughter sounded from across the table. I glanced over my menu and saw Carrie leaning into her mother as they looked at something on her mom's cell phone. Probably a photo. Their shoulders touched. The closeness jabbed me and I closed my menu and glanced away.

Fortunately Carrie gave her order to the waiter first, and since I liked everything she was having — escargot, steak, and Caesar salad — I ordered the same except for the appetizer. In my family we weren't allowed to order anything but the main course, so the addition of a salad was enough. That is, if we even went out to dinner. When was the last time?

Years ago. On Kat's sixth birthday. I remembered the exact day. Mom and Dad had a huge fight at the table and Kat started crying. They were fighting way back when, and it was always over money. They never seemed to care how we kids felt.

As we waited for our meals, Carrie and her mother bantered back and forth like best friends. I worked hard to keep my end of the conversation happening, but it was a struggle. Carrie kept trying to bring me in on every topic.

After the meal, as we walked outside, Carrie asked, "What are you up to tomorrow?"

"I dunno. Studying." Jonathon had some ergometer race that they were putting on for the parents, but he hadn't really invited me to come. From what he'd told me, they lined up the indoor rowing ergometers and they raced heats. Then they did semis and finals. It would have been fun to watch, but I wanted to be invited. Were we done before we even began?

I didn't have a practice or a game, which was totally strange. Usually the hours on a weekend were filled with basketball. I hated empty days.

"Really?" Carrie knocked me with her shoulder and I laughed. I hoped she couldn't hear how fake it was.

"It's not like you to study on a Saturday," she said.

"I have to," I groaned. "Math is so hard this year. I just don't get it. I'll have to call Parm. She always knows the answers."

"I'm going to watch Carrie's team perform their routines," piped up Carrie's mother. "Why don't you join me? I could use a friend to sit with."

"Sounds good," I answered. "Let's text tomorrow." At least it would give me something to do while *everyone* else was with their parents.

When I got back to my billet house, it was still and eerily quiet. And, of course, there was not a thing, not even a pencil, out of place. All the drawers in the house were organized and even the junk drawer in the kitchen had sections. One for pens and one for pencils, and if I mixed the two, Abigail would let me know. John and Abigail were good billets, but sometimes I longed for a house with a family instead of a couple so focused on their careers.

I went to the kitchen and grabbed a granola bar from the pantry. Then, because Abigail was gone, I took it to my room. Abigail hated it when I ate in my room and often searched my trash can for discarded wrappers. John didn't care, but he also didn't tell Abigail not to ride me so hard. Tonight she was gone, so I would leave the wrapper on my desk.

My phone rang just as I had changed into my flannel snowman pyjamas. I quickly picked it up, hoping it was

Jonathon. But when I looked at the number, I saw it was my sister Kat.

"Hey," I said, sitting on my bed. "What's up?"

"Not much. How'd your night go?"

I switched positions to sit cross-legged. At least one person in my family cared. "Personal best," I replied.

"Awesome! I wish I'd been there to watch."

"Me too," I said.

There was a pause for a moment before she said, "I've got a job at the coffee shop around the corner."

"I didn't work when I was your age," I said. "You should be concentrating on your marks." I paused. Anger boiled inside me. "I still can't believe Mom lost her life savings. How dumb could she be?"

"Harry was a con artist," said Kat. "It's not *all* Mom's fault."

"Of course it's her fault. If she hadn't been so desperate, she'd have some money and you wouldn't need to get a job *and* you could have flown out to see me play." Harry had been my mother's *third* boyfriend after she and my dad split, and he'd scammed her big-time. Unfortunately we kids were the losers in that deal.

Kat paused on the other end of the line, which was so unlike her. I waited for her to speak. Usually when she phoned, I could hardly talk because she wanted to talk trash about Mom. Why the silence now?

When I couldn't stand the still air any longer, I opened my mouth to speak, but she blurted out, "She has a new boyfriend."

"What?" I stood. My parents had split just over a year

ago while I was away at school. I had heard the news from thousands of miles away and could do nothing to help anyone but listen. I paced across the room. I swear flames were coming out the top of my head.

Kat didn't speak. So I did. "You're kidding, right?"

"I'm not," said Kat quietly.

I exhaled loudly and kept pacing. My parents had left me with a mess in the summer too; I had come home after school last year to complete chaos. Kat nattered at me, asking question after question, and nine-year-old Olive followed me everywhere. And my mom was out every night, leaving the house in sleazy clothing that I wouldn't wear if you paid me. She would sneak in the back door well after midnight, smelling of cigarettes and booze. Gross. Sometimes I waited up for her and told her how mad I was. Being a barfly had become more important to her than her daughters.

"How could she do this?" I barked. "Has she no pride? She just goes from one guy to the next."

"He seems nicer than the other ones," said Kat.

"Really, Kat?" I sighed and fell back on my bed and stared at the ceiling.

"Cut Mom some slack, Allie."

I sat up and squared my shoulders. "Are you kidding me? You're sticking up for her now after all she's done to us? To you? I can't believe you're on her side."

I could hear Kat breathing. Finally she said, "I'm not on anyone's *side*. Dad was a jerk to her."

"That doesn't excuse how she acts. She's our *mother.*"

"I really think she's trying harder. And honestly, this

new guy does seem okay. She's been so much happier. She's been with him for a few months now."

"A few months? And I'm just finding out now? Why didn't you tell me?"

"I knew you'd freak. He's a good guy, Allie."

Why was Kat talking like this? We'd always been a unit, a team. Two against one. Now it was as if she was leaving me out.

"Yeah, well, she was happy last time too until he left us with nothing. She's irresponsible."

"Come on, Allie."

"What is wrong with you, Kat? Have you got blinders on?"

"Dad doesn't give her a cent. Yeah, she made some bad choices but this is different."

"She's the adult in this situation! Not you. You sound like her psychologist. By the way, how is *Dad*?"

"I dunno. I haven't seen him since he left."

"And I'll never, mark my words, see him again," I said. My dad was a drunk and it was so disgusting that he liked girls who were barely older than me. What father does *that*?

"Yeah, me neither," said Kat. "If you met Mike, though, you'd like him. She's dressing better, and they go to dinner and the movies and on walks."

My breath caught in my throat. Just like a balloon being pricked, my anger deflated and my chest ached. "So," I said quietly, "she can go to dinner and the movies but she can't come see me play?"

"Let's talk about something else." Kat's words came out in a rush.

"O-kay." I was tired of the conversation anyway. "How's Olive?" I smiled when I said her name.

"Good. Still playing hockey and loving it. Still hanging with all the boys on her team and still being a tomboy. Mike goes to all her games and even gives her tips. She loves that. Dad never goes to see her play. She wants to go to Podium, like you."

"Is this Mike guy horning in on our family?" I closed my eyes. I could feel a headache coming on. "Kat, is Mom there? Maybe I should talk to her."

Another weird pause stretched from Halifax.

"Kat, where's Mom?" I asked.

"Mom and Mike went to Cape Breton for the weekend."

"She left you alone?"

"I'm sixteen, Allie. You babysat us when you were my age. Mom worked those crazy night shifts. I can manage the house for a weekend."

"Oh my gawd! This is crazy. When I took care of you guys, she didn't leave the city. She was at work. I knew where to find her. She shouldn't up and leave you and Olive for a *weekend*. What the hell is wrong with her?"

"I can do this, Allie. We don't need you. You're going places with your basketball."

I sighed. I had made the choice to come back to Podium knowing life was crappy at home. Kat usually called for help, but here she was, doing it all herself.

Kat and I talked for a few more minutes about nothing really, school and clothes and stuff, then hung up. I tossed my phone back and forth in my hand. Everything at home was changing. What could I do from so far away? Kat sounded way too grown up. And it was as if they'd forgotten about me, didn't need me anymore.

She'd even stuck up for Mom. That was a first. Why? Why would she do that?

But the worst of it all was that this Mike guy — Mr. New-and-Wonderful and probably another fraud — and Mom had gone to Cape Breton for a little lovefest on *Parents Weekend*. And she hadn't even phoned to ask me about my game!

My body started to shake. And suddenly I began to scream.

Loud. Louder.

I didn't muffle the noise because no one was home. No one. I was alone. I hated the feeling and it made me want to shrivel up and die. Finally I stopped screaming and wrapped my arms around myself to control my trembling body. The depressing emptiness I had felt after the game returned, only this time it was worse.

I flopped down on my bed and buried my face in the pillow. I bet Mom wouldn't miss me if I was dead. It would make her life easier. And then they started. The tears. Why didn't my mother care? Sobs racked my body.

CHAPTER THREE

I woke up Saturday morning and groaned. How was I going to get through this weekend? I didn't even have a practice today to take up time. *Bingo.* I could go shoot some baskets. Exercise was good for the endorphins. Hopefully the gym would be available.

I glanced at my phone, and when I saw I had no new calls or texts, I got up, pulled on grey sweats and a huge Podium sweatshirt, and headed to the kitchen. Abigail sipped her coffee as she sat at the table reading the finance section of the newspaper. During the week she only had time to read the news on her iPad.

"You want coffee?" She peered over the paper.

"Sounds good." I grabbed a glass mug. When I spilled a little coffee on the counter, I heard her voice behind me.

"Grab a cloth. Coffee stains."

I quickly snatched the dishcloth and cleaned up my mess. "No stain," I said.

Once I had my bowl of yogurt and fruit, I sat down across from Abigail. "Where's John?" I asked.

"Running."

I nodded. John was this tall, skinny guy who was smart, worked hard, and had a dry sense of humour. "When's his next marathon?" I asked.

"Three weeks from now. In Florida."

"Cool," I said. "Warm too."

I ate a few mouthfuls of yogurt, wondering if she would ask me about last night. But she didn't. I ate some more. Neither of us spoke. Finally I said, "I had a personal best last night."

Abigail folded the newspaper, placed it on the table, and smiled at me. "Good for you. When's your next game?"

"Friday night."

She picked up her phone and glanced at it. "I'm free," she said. "I'll come watch."

"That would be great," I said. "Thanks."

Being Parents Weekend and all, the school was open early. With my basketball under my arm — the equipment room would be locked so I had to bring my own ball — I headed directly to the gym. I breathed a sigh of relief when I saw there was no other team practicing. Not yet, anyway. The volleyball team played in the afternoon and would probably be here around noon. After downing a pain reliever for my knee, I dribbled toward the basket. In the empty gym the sound of the ball bouncing echoed off the concrete walls. To me it was like good music.

The gym had a distinct smell too. Sweat mixed with the scent of polished wood. Crazy as it seems, the waxy smell gave me great comfort, and if I had to compare it to anything, it would be the smell of home cooking, like fresh lobster and butter.

I jumped and took a shot. The ball bounced off the rim and I flew in for the rebound. I jumped again and this time I sank the ball. I scooped it up and practiced my dribbling: behind my back, between my legs, right hand, left hand. Dribbling was my weakest skill. Shooting was my best.

"Practice makes perfect, Allie," I said to myself. "Practice makes perfect."

I glanced at the clock. I would dribble for at least fifteen minutes.

And I did, bouncing the ball over and over, side to side, back and forth. I danced on my feet, my high-tops squeaking. Then faster. Faster.

I took off running, guiding the ball forward. *Control. Don't let the ball take control. You control the ball.*

I ran up and down the court. When fifteen minutes were up, my T-shirt was soaked in sweat. I wiped my face with a towel and looked at the basket. Now for my reward: shooting baskets.

Shooting for me didn't have a time limit because I could do it for hours. I always played a little game with myself. I would shoot one hundred baskets and count how many I got in. If I lost track of the count, I had to start over.

I started at the free-throw line and moved around the key. Nine, ten. Suddenly I heard Kat's words — *"Cut Mom some slack, Allie"* — and I missed the eleventh shot. And the twelfth. And the thirteenth. I kept going, but somewhere in the next five balls, I lost count.

Darn it. I would have to start at the beginning. Again I

moved to the top of the key. "Okay, Allie. Here we go. One hundred balls."

I shot, grabbed my rebound, and shot again. I moved outside the key and inside the key, and I even sank one from the three-point mark.

Thirty balls and I'd missed two.

"They go to dinner and the movies."

I lost count again. I grit my teeth and closed my eyes for a second.

"Stop. Just stop speaking to me!" I yelled. I opened my eyes, glanced around. Thankfully I was still alone. My stupid family haunted me.

"Try again, Allie," I said out loud. I had to do this.

Four more times I tried and the farthest I got was twelve baskets in fourteen shots before I lost count again. This was so stupid! I couldn't get Kat's voice out of my head. My family was messing with me even from thousands of miles away.

Discouraged, I stood at the top of the key to practice my free throws. I had sunk seven in a row when a voice sounded behind me.

"I thought you'd be home sleeping after your great game last night."

I turned and saw Parmita walking toward me. Not only was she a fantastic soccer goalie, she also had the highest marks in the school. Her goal was to be a doctor, a surgeon to be exact, and there was no doubt in anyone's mind that she would achieve that goal.

"You were there?" I asked.

"Of course I was. Your knee seemed okay last night."

She pointed to it. "Where's your brace?"

I wiped my face on the sleeve of my T-shirt. "Left it at home. Knee's fine." Parm was like a walking medical book. "What are you doing here? I thought your game was tomorrow."

"It is. Abigail said you'd gone to the gym."

"You dropped by?"

"Yeah. I tried calling but you didn't answer."

I nodded. "My phone's in the change room."

"You want to go for something to eat?"

"Love to," I said. "I'm starving."

Parm and I met at Nellie's, a funky restaurant that served breakfast all day and had the best eggs Benedict anywhere. We both closed our menus at the same time. "I thought you'd be with your parents," I said.

"I was. We had an early breakfast together, but they wanted to go to Banff and I didn't want to. I've got homework to do." She paused. "You played amazing last night."

I quickly glanced at her, trying to see if she was mad like Carrie had said last night. Nothing showed in her face so I guessed she was over it now. But that was so Parm. Hot and cold.

"Thanks," I said. "Hey, are you working on your math homework today?"

"Yeah, why? You need help?"

I nodded. "Yeah. Big-time."

Parm shrugged. "We could go to my place after we eat. Or yours."

I held up my thumb. "I'm in."

My phone on the table vibrated and I picked it up. When I saw the text from Carrie's mother, I slapped my forehead. "I totally forgot," I moaned. "I told Carrie's mom last night I would sit with her at the synchro practice today. I guess they're doing their routines for the parents."

Parm tried to smile but I could see the disappointment in her eyes. "You gotta do what you gotta do."

"It doesn't start until three. We could work for an hour or so."

Parm nodded. "That works for me."

Our food came and we remained silent as we both started to eat. After a few bites, I looked at Parm. "Hey," I said. "I hope you're not mad about me giving Carrie the rose last night."

Parm avoided my gaze but shook her head. "Of course I'm not mad."

"It's just that Carrie and I have known each other a long time and I'm friends with her mother too. She's taken me out a lot." I forged ahead with the excuse.

Parm put her fork down and it clanged against the plate. "Allie, I'm not mad, okay? It's not a big deal. I'm glad you have someone like Carrie's mother in your life. I wish your mother could have come."

"I don't care," I said.

"I think you do," she said gently.

"I don't, okay?" I shovelled in a mouthful of eggs and hollandaise.

My place was closer, so Parm and I met there. We went right to my room and got down to business. No matter where I sat, Parmita always seemed to sit beside me so our legs or shoulders or arms touched. Was I imagining that I could feel her warm breath on my skin?

We worked through a few of the easy problems, then started on one that I just didn't understand. Ever patient, Parm went over and over the formula with me, breaking the question down into small steps.

"Do you understand what I'm saying here?" She pointed to the numbers on the page. In just ten minutes, she had explained a problem that I had spent an hour trying to solve two nights ago.

"Yeah! I get it." I held up my hand and she slapped it.

"Thanks," I said. "You're a lifesaver."

She stood up. "You better get going. You don't want to be late."

I glanced at my phone to see the time. When I saw that Jonathon had texted me just to say hi, I quickly picked it up and texted him back, asking how his erg test had gone.

"took notes from you last night at your game and killed it," he replied.

I laughed and texted him back: "good on ya"

"Who you texting?" Parm asked.

"Jonathon." I laughed again at his second response, which was a funny note on how the guy ahead of him kept farting during his erg test. I fired off a funny note back. We liked sending funny notes to each other.

His next note said: "dinner tonight with my parents?"

"You're not seriously thinking of going out with him?" Parm frowned at me.

I sent off a quick one word: "sure."

Then I said to Parm, "He's super fun."

"Be careful, Allie. You're always falling for the wrong guy."

This time it was my turn to frown. "How do you know he's the wrong guy?" Could she be jealous?

Parm grabbed her parka from the back of the chair. "I know you better than you think. Have fun at Carrie's rehearsal. Are you going out with her and her mother again tonight?"

"Actually, no," I replied.

She tucked her hair behind her ear and her face suddenly softened. "You, um, want to go out with me and my parents? They'd love to meet you."

"I can't," I mumbled. "I've got other plans." Because of her comment about Jonathon, I didn't want to tell her I was going out with *him*.

CHAPTER FOUR

"So, Allie," said Jonathon's mother, "you had an amazing game last night."

We were at this high-class steak house in downtown Calgary. When I'd walked in, I immediately felt under-dressed, even though I'd worn a skirt, turtleneck, and boots. The tables were set with a ton of silverware, way too many glasses, linen napkins, and flickering candles.

"Thanks," I replied, my face heating. "Our entire team played well."

One thing Coach Cathy drilled into us was that every player was only as good as her teammates.

"Spoken like a true captain," said his father. He glanced down at his menu. "What's everyone having?"

The items on the menu were really expensive and I immediately looked for the cheapest dish. I could order the six-ounce filet or I could wait until Jonathon ordered and just order the same thing.

"What are you having, Allie? Order anything you want."

"Maybe a steak," I said. When I glanced down at the menu again, I noticed that none of the meals came with anything. You had to order all the sides separately.

"How about an appetizer?" His mother looked at me over the rim of her reading glasses. "I like the looks of the calamari or maybe that lobster pâté with fennel. I love lobster."

"I don't need an appetizer," I said, sipping my water.

She looked down at her menu again. "Oh, look, Rick, they have lamb. And, ohhh, they have mussels." A big smile on her face, she looked up from her menu at me again. "They have that wonderful restaurant in Halifax with the mussel bar and fantastic lobster."

"Three Fishermen," I said. "It's one of my favourites."

We used to go there, well, sometimes, when I was younger, but only on really special occasions. I doubted we would ever go out again unless . . . I didn't want to think of someone like *Mike* taking us out as a family.

"Do you eat a lot of lobster in Halifax?" Jonathon asked, putting his linen napkin on his lap.

I followed Jonathon and put my napkin on my lap. "Yeah. We have big lobster festivals in the spring. It's fun. Everyone wears a silly plastic bib and we just eat as much lobster as we can. My max is like five."

"Five?" Jonathon laughed and playfully jabbed me in the ribs. Then he leaned into me so our shoulders touched. He smelled amazing, sort of like musk and wood. His biceps bulged through his shirt.

"I'm always looking for new lobster recipes," said Jonathon's mother, obviously unaware that her son was flirting with me.

"I make a mean lobster roll," I said.

"You cook?" Jonathon asked, lifting his eyebrows before putting his arm around the back of my chair. "You don't strike me as someone who'd have culinary skills."

I playfully slapped his arm. "Ha ha. I do most of the cooking at home."

"Good for you, Allie," said Jonathon's mother.

"Especially for my sisters," I said. My face flushed. I immediately lowered my head and stared at my menu. Jonathon and his parents couldn't find out anything about my life in Halifax. Nothing. I had said that without thinking and I didn't want Jonathon to even know that my parents were divorced. And I certainly didn't want him knowing that my mother had an ex-boyfriend who had ripped her off. Or that I cooked for my sisters because my mother didn't, and all summer long I did all the grocery shopping and I even cut coupons to make the grocery money last longer.

Jonathon's mother saved me by pulling out her Black-Berry. "I would love to have that recipe. Will you send it to me? Give me your phone number and I'll text you."

She wanted the recipe from me? She was so nice!

Jonathon leaned into me and whispered, "She thinks she's cool because she can text."

"I heard that, Jonathon, and I've been texting for years."

I yanked out my phone. "I'd love to send you the re-cipe. I have mussel recipes too." Again I just talked without thinking. *Big mouth, Allie.* "My, uh, mom, loves mussels so we, uh, eat a lot of mussels and fish and stuff like that. The market is on every Saturday morning and it's always fresh. We do a mother-daughter day there. It's fun."

My mother hated the market, said it smelled. I loved it and went every Saturday by myself to pick up food for the week.

After exchanging numbers, we got back to figuring out what we wanted to eat. When the waiter came to the table to take the orders, I asked for the calamari to start and a small steak. I let Jonathon's parents worry about the side dishes. I closed my menu because I didn't want to think about the bill.

"So tell me about your plans for next year," said Jonathon's mother as she buttered a roll.

"I have a scholarship for Duke," I said.

"That's impressive," said his father. "Isn't there some women's professional basketball league in the States?"

I nodded. "That's my dream."

"Well, dream big or go home," said his mother.

"Mo-om." Jonathon rolled his eyes. "You say the most embarrassing things sometimes."

She laughed and animatedly waved her hands in the air. "That's what we moms are supposed to do. It keeps you kids on your toes." She looked at me and winked. "I bet your mother does the same thing as me."

I faked a laugh. "Oh yeah," I said.

"You can keep everyone on their toes all right." His father laughed. He wagged his finger at Jonathon. "You left me alone with her. You weren't supposed to leave for another two years."

Jonathon's mother leaned over and kissed his father on the cheek. "You love me. Just admit it."

The light banter between Jonathon and his parents

continued throughout the meal, and I found myself being drawn into the warm family atmosphere. I liked it. A lot. Not once did I feel excluded either. In every conversation, they asked something about me, but the best part was that when I talked, they listened. Jonathon reminded me of his mother, in personality and facial features. They both had thick, sandy-blond hair and these gorgeous smiles with perfect teeth and sparkly eyes. But she was tiny in build, and Jonathon, with his height and broad shoulders, was built just like his father.

We finished eating by nine and Jonathon's dad had the bill paid by nine ten.

"We have to get you home, Jonathon" said his mother. "You have an early workout tomorrow." She gestured to Jonathon to get my coat from the rack.

As he moved close to me to help me put it on, I could feel his body heat. I stuck out my arms and he slipped on the coat. His warm breath on my neck made me flush and shiver at the same time. "Thanks," I said shyly.

"Anytime." He met my eyes and I could have melted on the spot.

At the door of the restaurant, Jonathon's mother gave me a hug. "It was so nice to meet you, Allie."

"You too," I replied.

Jonathon opened the door and a cold wind blew in, followed by snow. His mother frowned and turned to me. "Are you going to be all right, honey, driving home in this snow?"

"I'll be fine." I smiled at her. "Thanks for worrying."

I was in my pyjamas, ready for bed, when my phone rang. Hoping it was Jonathon asking if I made it home okay, I snatched it off my night table. When I looked at the number, I saw that it was my mom.

I groaned before I answered it. "Hi," I mumbled.

"Allie, hi, it's Mom."

"I know. Your number comes up on my phone." I sat on the end of my bed and leaned against the wall.

"Oh, okay," she said. "How are you?"

"Good," I answered.

Silence.

Was she at least going to ask me about Parents Weekend? I sure as heck wasn't going to give her any information or any clues. I wanted to see if she'd remember on her own.

Of course, as I figured, the silence lingered like a bad odour. Did she want *me* to ask how *she* was? That was generally how all our conversations went, all about her. I wondered if Kat had told her that she'd told me about Mike.

Finally, Mom asked, "How's school?"

"Good." I twirled my finger through my frizzy hair.

"I've been meaning to send you some money," she said. "But I'm a little short this month."

I sighed. We always talked about money. Last summer, when she got scammed, she said she couldn't afford to send me back to school. So I'd gone online and paid for my own ticket to Calgary with some of my summer savings. "I have enough," I said. "Don't worry about me."

My meals and accommodation were paid for, so all I needed at Podium was spending money. I had worked as a waitress last summer in a bistro and had made good tips, plus I'd taught at some basketball camps. My flights between Halifax and Calgary were supposed to be my parents' responsibility. When Thanksgiving had rolled around, I'd told her I had to practice. In December I'd managed to do a bit of work at an elementary school, teaching basketball, and they had paid me cash. I'd used that money to help Mom pay for my Christmas ticket. Now she had this Mike guy and was going to dinner and the movies and away for the weekend. So how could she still be moaning about money?

"Okay," she said. "That's good." It bugged me that she sounded so relieved. Sometimes I felt sorry for her, but not this time. I guess for once I just wanted her to say she was *worried* about me. Or that she had saved some money for me, that she had worked a few overtime shifts to buy my ticket or send me a hundred dollars. That's all. Jonathon's mother barely knew me and she was worried about me driving home in the snow.

"How's your knee?" She broke the silence again.

"Fine," I answered. Again the undertone was there. She didn't really care about my knee, only about the medical costs. "If you're worried about paying for an MRI for me," I said, "I don't need one. Knee's back to normal."

"That's good," she said.

I glanced at my knee. When I'd injured it last year playing basketball, it had healed just fine, but when I was in a car accident, I'd reinjured it badly enough that I should have had an MRI. But she didn't have enough money for that. So I had rested the knee and iced it and the swelling had subsided.

Again there was this awkward silence on the phone. I

only let it last a few moments because . . . because I just couldn't stand it any longer.

"By the way," I said. "I had a personal best last night. On opening night of *Parents Weekend.*" I wanted to be mean to her, and it was wrong, but I didn't know how to stop myself. "I gave *your* rose to my friend Carrie. All the other players on my team gave the rose to their mothers except Karen, because her mother died. So she gave the rose to her grandmother."

"Allie, I'm sorry I wasn't there," Mom said softly. "I just couldn't get a cheap flight."

"Whatever."

"I tried. I really did."

"Obviously not hard enough," I muttered.

"Allie, come on now. You know what happened. Right now I live paycheque to paycheque and I don't have the luxury of extras. I have to start saving now to be able to pay for your flight home in June. Your father doesn't give me any support."

"Maybe I won't come home." I straightened my back. "I'm sure I could get a job in Calgary. So don't worry about *saving* for me."

I could hear her breathing on the other end. I closed my eyes. Had I made her cry?

"You didn't even call me on Friday night after my game," I said. My throat clogged. I wanted to be the one to cry. Not her.

"I was going to," she said.

Tears pricked my eyes. I shook my head. I had to be strong. "Why didn't you?"

"I was really busy, Allie."

"Why don't you just be honest with me? You forgot, Mom. Because you were with what's-his-name. Oh, right, *Mike*. Kat told me all about your new boyfriend. So has *Mike* gone home now or something? Or did Kat tell you to call me? And why would you leave Kat to babysit for a weekend? What kind of mother does that?"

"Allie, I'm sorry. I'm trying."

"Obviously not hard enough." This time I didn't mutter the words. I spoke them loud and clear.

CHAPTER FIVE

Math on Monday was a breeze, thanks to Parmita's help over the weekend. Good thing too because I was having a hard time concentrating. I kept thinking of my stupid family and tapping my pencil on the desk. Carrie turned around and glared at me.

"Gahhh," I muttered.

She narrowed her eyes at me and whispered, "What's going on?"

"Crap."

She nodded and turned to face front again, but only because the teacher was giving us the eye. Class ended and thankfully it was time for lunch. Carrie, Parmita, and I walked down the hall toward the cafeteria.

"How's Jonathon?" Carrie bumped me with her hip, which hit me about mid-thigh.

I held up my thumb. "So far so good."

"So he's not the problem?"

I shook my head. "I don't wanna talk now. It's just my stupid family. I wanna eat." I bumped her, knocking her off balance, which made us both burst out laughing. Parmita shook her head and walked ahead of us.

"You're right," Carrie whispered. "Intense."

"Yup. But boy, did she help me with my math." Now that Parm was out of earshot, I said, "Hey, I met Jonathon's parents the other night."

"Wow, you guys are moving fast. Meeting the parents is huge."

"We went out to this really classy restaurant. I think they're like super rich. But so nice." I yanked my phone out of my pocket. "I've been texting back and forth with his mother."

"Excuse me?" Carrie lifted one side of her mouth and made a funny face. "With his *mother*? What about?"

"Recipes."

Carrie burst out laughing. "Seriously? Recipes? If you're doing that, you're like every mother's dream. But getting in with a guy's mother so soon is crazy stuff, girl."

"He's a good guy." Out of the corner of my eye, I saw him turning a corner up ahead and going in the same direction we were. My heart started racing.

"There he is," I said to Carrie, the words tumbling out of my mouth. I shot her a look, my one-eyebrow-up look. "Don't you dare tell him I'm texting his mom. Come on, let's catch up with him."

We picked up our pace, my legs taking one stride to Carrie's two.

She giggled. "I'm going to have a heart attack if you don't slow down."

Seconds later we were walking beside Jonathon. "Hey," I said, immediately slowing down and trying to act cool.

"Hey," he said back. His shoulder rubbed against mine and I shivered.

"You going to eat?" I asked. Beside me, Carrie rolled her eyes as if to say, *Duh, of course he's going to eat. He's on his way to the cafeteria.*

"Yeah," he replied, oblivious to the silent communication between Carrie and me. "Not for long, though," he said. "I got math this aft and it's killing me."

"What unit you on?"

"Trig."

I held up my thumb. "Need my help?" Beside me Carrie covered her mouth and looked away. I wasn't known for my genius math skills. "Parm tutored me," I stated. "I get it now."

"Sure. I'll take any help I can get."

"I'll catch up with you guys in there," said Carrie. "I need to talk to Nathan for a second."

"KK," I said.

As soon as Carrie was gone, Jonathon took my hand. I liked that he wanted to hold my hand in the hall. It made me feel special.

"Thanks again for inviting me to dinner," I said shyly.

He squeezed my hand. "My mother couldn't stop talking about you. There's only me and my brother and Dad, so she always feels outnumbered. She likes it when there's another female around."

"My family's the opposite," I said. "I have two sisters."

"Your dad must feel like my mom." He grinned. "She always says too much testosterone, and I bet your dad says too much estrogen."

"Yeah," I said, faking a laugh, "that is sooo true. My dad

always says that." The lie plummeted out of my mouth. I wanted him to think I had a family like his.

We sat down at our usual place in the cafeteria with some of our usual gang. Jonathon sat beside me, and when our thighs touched, it sent tingles up and down my body. It was all I could do to eat. It was a typical lunch, where Nathan and Quinn acted like they were in kindergarten, wrestling and playing silly games. Parmita studied her notes and ate her lunch at the same time. Jax wasn't around because he had left for California on a snowboarding trip, and Aaron and Kade were also gone on a hockey road trip. Podium was such a different school that way. Because we were all athletes, we were excused from attending class when we had tournaments or meets or competitions. The teachers didn't penalize us, but actually gave us work and helped us, which was the best part.

Halfway through lunch, Jonathon opened his math book. "I have to look at this."

"Sure," I said, leaning close to him. I glanced at Parm and saw her just shake her head and get to her feet.

I didn't care how she felt about Jonathon and me. I turned back to him. "Which one you stuck on?"

We only got one question done before lunch ended. It wasn't enough for Jonathon to grasp the entire concept.

"You want to get together tonight?" I asked. "You could come over." I knew Abigail and John were working late tonight so it would be perfect.

Practice was definitely the highlight of my day. Well, that and Jonathon saying he *could* come over. I raced to the change room when last class was over, wanting to be first on the court. My club coach back in Halifax had drilled that into me.

I grabbed a ball from the rack and started warming up. Nothing felt better than being on the court.

Well, maybe there was something else that *might* feel better. Sex. I was still a virgin. I ran around the court, dribbling. Was Jonathon the one?

I ran forward and backward and dribbled with both hands. I had been playing basketball since I was five. I'd started shooting hoops at the school down the street and sometimes I was there until dark. Every year I tried out for the school team and every year I played with girls way older than I was. It helped that I was so tall. When I got the letter to come to Podium, my parents were totally confused, thinking it was going to cost them money. When they found out it was a scholarship, I was allowed to attend. I left in grade ten.

I would never have got my scholarship to Duke if I hadn't come to Podium.

"Hi, Allie." Marla jumped and swished the ball through the hoop.

"Nice one," I said. "I can't wait until Friday. I hope we work on zone again today."

"Me too," replied Marla.

Soon we were joined by the rest of the team and the sound of basketballs thumping the floor echoed through the gym. We all dribbled and shot and dribbled and shot. Until Coach Cathy blew the whistle.

We moved to centre court. "I hope you guys had a nice,

relaxing weekend," said Coach Cathy. "I was extremely pleased with your execution on Friday night and your composure with such a big crowd. This weekend we have two games. Friday will be a tough one and Sunday will be easier as the team is definitely weaker. I would like to give some playing time to the second string in our second weekend game."

I glanced at some of the second-string players and held up my thumb. As captain I needed to stay positive with them and keep letting them know their time would come if they worked hard.

"Okay," said Coach Cathy. "Today will be a conditioning day since we were off all weekend. Everyone line up on the baseline."

Of course there were a few murmurs of complaint, but I led everyone to the line. Once we were all lined up, I looked up and down the line and said, "Let's do this. Put everything into it and work through any pain."

Coach Cathy blew her whistle and I sprinted forward. When the whistle blew, I turned around and ran backwards. The whistle blew two more times before we hit the end. I doubled over to catch my breath.

"Fifteen seconds' rest!" boomed Coach Cathy.

When I had my breathing in check, I shook out my knee.

We did the length of the gym twenty times and we had thirty seconds for running and rest. By the tenth time, our running had slowed and the rest was down to about ten seconds. In between I bent over and rubbed my knee. When we hit the twentieth time, we had no more than one second to rest.

Finally the drill ended and I went over to the bench to get some water.

"That one's a killer," said Lydia.

"Sooo hard," I replied.

"You win every time," she said.

"I've got longer legs than you."

She attempted a smile. "That you do."

Coach Cathy was on a mission, and after a quick water break, she ran us through conditioning exercises for another thirty minutes.

"That's enough," she finally said. "Get some water and meet back on the court. We're going to do some zone work today. First string, you'll start on offence. Second string defence, then we'll switch up."

While everyone towelled their faces and gulped water, I walked over to Coach Cathy. "Can I take a real quick pee break?"

"Yeah, but hustle."

"Gotcha."

I ran into the change room, quickly found my purse, pulled out a bottle of pain relievers, and took three. Two were never enough. Back in the gym, I swigged my water and took my spot on offence. I looked at Marla, Lydia, Karen, and Breanne. This year, we'd really started to gel as a line. I could honestly say it was the best line I'd ever played on.

"Marla, bring it down," called out Coach Cathy.

Marla bounced the ball and the rest of us ran down the court. On my first pivot, I could feel a dull ache in my knee. I kept pivoting, shuffling, and moving to get open.

Marla bounced the ball to me and I made a few dekes with my shoulders, passing off to Lydia. We kept moving the ball around the key.

Soon I knew the pain relievers had kicked in. When the ball came to me and I could see a lane open, I took a stride, jumped, and sank the ball.

By the end of practice, I was exhausted. That had been the hardest practice we'd had in a long time. I threw my towel around my neck and started heading to the change room when I heard Coach Cathy call my name.

I turned.

"Can I talk to you for a sec?"

"Sure," I replied.

She put her hand on my shoulder. "How are you doing?"

"Good," I said.

"You're okay after Parents Weekend?"

I sucked in a deep breath and exhaled. "Yeah, I'm fine." I shrugged.

"Life sometimes gives us obstacles. Don't give up on your dreams."

"I won't." I paused but just for a few seconds. "I don't know what I'd do without Podium, though. And you. And my basketball."

She smiled at me. "You're going far. I have total faith you'll have great success at Duke next year. You've got what it takes, mentally and physically. One day I fully expect to see you playing pro."

"I appreciate your support," I said, feeling oddly shy. I guess I'd never had a coach I respected as much as Cathy.

"By the way," she continued, "I really like how you're leading the team. You're encouraging the younger girls and I've had a lot of them talk to me about how great you are with them. That means a lot to the program."

"Thanks," I said. "I won't let you down."

"It's not all about me, Allie. It's about you too. And know that I will be here for you. Anytime you want to talk, I'm available."

For some reason I reached out and hugged her. I'd never hugged a coach before. It didn't last long because suddenly I felt really awkward. "Thanks again," I mumbled before I made my way to the change room.

CHAPTER SIX

Jonathon showed up on my doorstep at seven, right on time. By his wet hair, which was covered in little ice crystals, he'd obviously just showered. I touched his hair. "I thought your workout started at three thirty. Did you *just* finish?"

He touched his hair too and nodded. "We had this killer weight workout. I can barely lift my arms. I can't wait to get on the water again. It's so much easier and way more fun."

I ushered him in, and when he slipped out of his shoes, I didn't bother lining them up. Abigail wasn't home, so what did it matter? "When will that be?" I asked. "Calgary has crap weather for you rowers."

"March. We'll do a two-week training camp in Victoria on Elk Lake and another one in April. And if there's still ice on the water here in May, we'll go back to Victoria."

I led him through the living room to the kitchen. It was definitely too early in the relationship to take him to my bedroom, although I was tempted. He smelled fresh, like soap, and he looked darn good in his jeans and T-shirt. "When is your big meet again?" I asked.

"June. In Ontario. We have to beat Ridley College. We also have some big regattas in the States just before the Canadian Schoolboy. So lots of travel in the spring."

He snuck up behind me and wrapped his arms around my waist. "But let's not talk about that now."

I leaned back into him, pressing against his hard chest. I let my head fall and my eyes close. He blew warm air in my ear. "That tickles," I giggled. I turned to face him.

We looked into each other's eyes for a few moments before he pressed his lips to mine. Electricity charged through me as I lifted my arms and ran my fingers through his hair. He moaned at my touch and pulled me closer, wrapping his arms around me, resting his hands on my butt. He pulled me into him and we were so close there wasn't even room for a piece of paper between us. Heat flowed through me and I trembled, but his strong, comforting arms held me up.

When the kiss ended, we stayed wrapped together for a few moments, just gazing into each other's eyes. His looked like warm pools of blue with little flecks of fun.

"Can't we forget about math?" he whispered. His eyes crinkled in the corners.

"Sure. I'm game for that." I ran a finger up and down his chest. "But what about the test?" I teased.

He kissed the tip of my nose. "Ahhh. Math always ruins the fun. But you're right." He shook his head and pulled away just a bit. "If I fail, I can't go to Schoolboy. Coach told me that."

I touched his cheek with my fingertips. "Then we'd better get started," I whispered.

We sat at the table, but pulled our chairs close. For an hour we worked on math problems, our heads bowed to the books, our shoulders and thighs touching. Every part of his body on mine made me tremble inside. It was very hard to focus.

Of course, because we were both starving after the hour was up, I made nachos and cheese and we ate and talked. The conversation worked with no effort and when I heard the garage door opening, I glanced at the kitchen clock on the stove. Wow! Where had the time gone? I stood up.

"That must be Abigail," I said. I quickly picked up the salsa jar and put it in the fridge. Next, the dishes. I took them to the sink, rinsed them off, and stuck them in the dishwasher, all the while listening to the sounds on the other side of the door, in the garage. I thought about Jonathon's shoes at the front entrance.

He came up behind me and wrapped his arms around my waist. "Are you going to get in trouble for me being here?" He breathed into my ear.

"I just have to leave the kitchen clean."

"I can help," he offered.

I turned and kissed him quickly, then handed him a dishcloth. "Wipe the table down."

Yikes. Time ran out. Abigail walked through the door before Jonathon had time to wipe the crumbs off the table.

"Hello," she said, eyeing Jonathon as she hung up her keys on a hook by the door.

Jonathon immediately stepped forward and held out his hand. "Hi. I'm Jonathon Muse."

Abigail shook his hand. "Pleased to meet you, Jonathon."

Her eyes narrowed as if she was assessing him.

I held my breath, waiting for her to mention the little pieces of nacho chips on the table. Was that why she was scrutinizing him? She thought I had brought home a slob?

Of course I was totally shocked when she asked, "Are you related to Peter Muse?"

Inside, I breathed this gigantic sigh of relief.

"That's my dad," said Jonathon. "How do you know him?"

Abigail smiled. "I've worked with him on a few projects. I've seen your photo in his office in Victoria. You're a rower."

If I could have yelled *yes!* and pumped my fist in the air, I would have. I discreetly took the cloth from Jonathon and wiped the table, making sure no crumbs hit the floor. When I glanced up, however, Abigail wasn't even looking at me. She was still captivated by Jonathon.

"Your dad is a wonderful businessman," she said, shrugging off her coat.

Bonus. Off the hook. Abigail liked Jonathon. I felt like singing.

The week passed by in a blur, what with preparing for the game on Friday and seeing Jonathon every spare moment we had. Our relationship seemed to be moving fast, like really fast, and for once I was chilling and letting it flow without trying to stop it. With every other boyfriend, I'd worked hard to make sure the relationship didn't move too quickly, but with this one, I was plunging in. Plunging in deep.

And it seemed like he was joining me for the ride.

Could we actually be falling *in love?* Was this it?

I talked to my sister once during the week and my mother not at all. She had called but I didn't call her back. She wasn't up on the texting game yet, because she pretended she didn't know how, so I didn't have to go that route with her. I had begged her to try so we could communicate that way, but all my efforts hadn't worked. What would she talk to me about anyway? Money? Mike? Thanks, but no thanks. Even Kat was making me crazy with her Mike-praise and her I'm-mature-now attitude. If they didn't need me, then I didn't need them.

True to her word, Abigail came to my game on Friday night. When I was warming up, I looked at the stands and saw that she and John were sitting with Jonathon. I was secretly thrilled. Carrie was out of town at a competition and Parm sat with her soccer friends.

Coach Cathy called us in and we huddled around her, listening to the game plan.

"This is a big physical team," she said. "They're tough and extremely rough. They play hard one to one and will stick on you and not let go. They'll invade your space and try to push you off the ball, and if the ref isn't looking, they'll play dirty. So keep your cool."

"I'm ready." Breanne was the first one to put her fist in the middle. I had to smile. This would be her type of game.

We all put in our fists, did our Podium cheer, then Lydia, Breanne, Karen, Marla, and I took to the floor, while the second string went to the bench. Often during a game,

Coach Cathy would substitute the second string in one by one, making sure they all got some playing time. Tonight she told them she wasn't sure how much court time they'd see, but on Sunday she repeated, when we played a weaker team, they were all starting.

I took my position at centre and went into my crouch. The ref threw the ball in the air and I jumped, touched it, and felt a knee pushing on my knee. Hard. Coming down, I almost lost my balance. No foul was called.

That's enough of that, I thought. I looked the player who'd kneed me in the eye and curled my lip. Players like her would tromp all over you if they knew you were the least bit intimidated. She gave me a saucy look back and I took off running.

Faster than her, I outran her to the hoop and called out to Marla. Marla threw me a long, perfect pass and I smashed the ball through the hoop.

"That'll teach you," I said to the girl from the opposing team when I ran by her.

As a team we took off down the court to play defence, with Lydia and Breanne playing high. Not only was Breanne the toughest player on our team, she was also the strongest, which was a great combo. She weighed in around 180 and was six feet tall. As the other team bounce-passed back and forth, Breanne watched eagerly until she saw her moment; then she pounced and intercepted. Lydia, Marla, Karen, and I stopped sharply, our shoes squeaking on the floor, and took off back toward their zone to grab the re-bound, if there was one.

Breanne was trailed by their two forwards, and when she

did her layup, a big girl, bigger and broader than Breanne, leaped up with her. I saw the shoulder lean and the girl purposely try to knock Breanne sideways. Breanne shot anyway, the ball hitting the backboard and rebounding out. I jumped and grabbed the rebound just as Breanne fell to the floor with the opposing player on top of her. I shot just as the whistle blew. I missed and the ball went flying out of bounds.

Arms and legs were tangled on the floor and Breanne pushed the girl. "Get off me," she growled.

I watched the ref's hand motions, wondering if he was going to call a double foul because of Breanne's retaliation, but he handed out an offensive foul to the other team. The girl glared at the ref and mumbled obscenities under her breath. We all took our places on the key. With attitude, Breanne stood at the top of the key, at the foul line, and I could tell by the smirk on her face she was taunting the girl. I noticed that her cheeks were blotchy red, a telltale sign she was fuming mad. She made both her shots and again we took off down the court.

This time instead of going for the pass, hoping for an interception, Breanne stepped right in front of the player, blocking her from running. The whistle blew. Breanne got an illegal block foul. As we walked to our key, Breanne and the girl had an exchange, and I could only guess what they said to each other. I'm sure the F-bomb and the B-word were mingled in with a few other choice words. I glanced at the clock. Lots of time still left in this quarter. Breanne might not make it. She had one foul and could easily rack up more if she didn't calm down. It was early in the game. I looked at the bench. Was Coach Cathy going to sub her out to give her time to cool down? Jacquie, Breanne's guard replacement, wasn't up and stripping down, so I guessed not. The fact was, if Coach Cathy did sub, Jacquie could be eaten and spit out by that girl. We called her Jolly Jacquie because she was always so positive on the bench and didn't have Breanne's killer instinct.

By the time the quarter was up, Breanne already had three fouls and the score was 14–13 for them.

"Control your emotions out there," said Coach Cathy when we were on the bench.

"I wanna punch her," Breanne whispered to me.

"Well, don't, okay?" I whispered back.

Halftime over, we took to the floor. At the jump ball, I was ready for the knee and I got my elbow ready. We both sprang up and I used my elbow to push her off me and to get the ball to Lydia. Again, no foul was given. The refs were letting a lot slide. This could get ugly.

Lydia dribbled, playing it safe. Lydia was a clean, more cautious player, than either Breanne or me, and because of that she rarely made mistakes. She worked on precision. She passed to Karen, who passed to Marla, who passed to me. I dribbled, pivoted, saw Breanne, and sent her a chest pass. Usually Breanne made sharp, quick passes but this time she held on to the ball and dribbled. Effectively too. Her shadow tried to slap at the ball and Breanne just moved it from hand to hand, testing her.

The girl pushed forward and tried to grab the ball but got Breanne's hand. The whistle blew and the girl shoved Breanne. The ball fell to the floor and Breanne pushed the girl back. "What is your problem?" she snapped.

"Take this, bitch." The girl gave Breanne another shove. *Push. Push. Push. Push.*

Punch! Breanne plowed the girl in the face. The girl punched Breanne back. They grabbed on to each other and started to really fight.

Marla jumped into the action. So did a girl from their team. I also ran over and tried to pull Marla out of the fight. Both refs ran over, but it was too late. Blood was dripping on the floor. Breanne had socked her good.

The refs pulled them apart. The crowd cheered like crazy, and when the ref held up his hands, he had to shout to be heard. "Fighting foul. Game suspension." Both Breanne and the girl were being ejected from the game. I groaned because after the game, there would be follow-ups, and my guess was that Breanne would be out for more than just this game.

Breanne stalked off the court, grabbed her towel, and headed for the change room.

Coach Cathy screamed from the bench, "That girl's been antagonizing my player all game!"

The ref looked at the bench and pointed at Coach Cathy. "Technical foul."

She slammed her notebook down and motioned for Jacquie to disrobe. Within seconds, Jacquie was running onto the court. I grabbed her by the shoulders and looked her square in the face. "Calm and cool, you can do this." Then I slapped her on the bum. "Let's go. Let's rack up the points."

When the game ended, we hadn't quite racked up the points, but we did win the game by a score of 51–50. After our team huddle, where Coach Cathy apologized for her temper, I hugged Jacquie. "You were awesome."

"Thanks, Allie." We slapped hands.

"Come on," I said. "Let's go talk to bruiser."

CHAPTER SEVEN

Jonathon was waiting for me after the game and his face was one huge grin. "Now that was a basketball game!"

"So crazy," I said. "I've never been in a game like that before. Ever."

"Girls fighting. Unbelievable." He laughed. "That was highly entertaining. The best we can do in my sport is have boat crashes."

"Where are John and Abigail?" I glanced around but couldn't see them. Off in the corner, though, I saw Parmita and as soon as we made eye contact, I lifted my hand and waved to her. It took her a second to acknowledge the gesture, but when she did, she started walking toward us.

"They left," Jonathon said in answer to my question.

"Oh. They said they would meet me after the game."

"They told me to tell you they were starving. I think they were heading out for a late bite to eat. Speaking of food, you hungry?"

"Would you mind going out with a few of the girls from my team?" I asked. In the change room before the game, Marla had planned for some of us to go out to a pizza place close to the school. Some were bringing boyfriends, so I thought it would be okay to bring Jonathon. Was he my boyfriend? Could I call him that yet?

He shrugged. "Why not?" Then he grinned again. "I could get some fighting tips."

I playfully punched his shoulder just as Parmita appeared beside me.

"Hey Parm," I said.

"Hi Parm," said Jonathon. "Do you guys fight in soccer too?"

Parmita laughed and I was relieved. "Breanne slugged her," said Parm, shaking her head. "When I played with the boys in Saskatchewan, we once had a brawl. But never when I played with girls."

I held up my hands. "Enough about the fight. I gotta shower." I glanced at Jonathon. "You wanna wait for me? Or meet me there?"

"I'll wait."

I started to walk toward the change room and Parmita followed. "I can't believe what happened in your game," she said.

"I know. Breanne will probably be out for a few games."

"How's the knee holding up?"

"Great."

She eyed me. "You're limping."

"I'll ice it." Just because she wanted to go to medical school didn't mean she could take me on as her project.

"Who was the sub?"

"Jacquie. She's in grade eleven."

Parm nodded. "She did a good job."

I nodded. "Yeah. It's hard to sub in for Breanne."

"You going out with Jonathon again?"

I eyed Parm. "Why are you asking so many questions?"

She shrugged. "I'm your friend."

Something was up with her, I could tell. *Could the rumours be true? Did she want to be more than a friend?*

I bumped her to lighten the mood. "Oh my gawd! I forgot to tell you. I saw this gorgeous grad dress the other day."

"I was thinking I'd go in a suit," she said.

Shocked, I glanced at her. Parm had always said she didn't want to go to graduation. Now she wanted to go in a suit? *Was she going to ask me?* I held up my fingers and crossed them. "I so want Jonathon to ask me," I said.

I showered quickly and tossed my hair because blow-drying it was out of the question. That beauty technique only worked when I was going to straighten it, which I only did on special occasions when I had time. Tonight Jonathon was waiting for me. I almost giggled. He could wait but I wasn't going to wait forever with him. No way. I shuddered, thinking of lying in his arms, against his bare chest.

Yup, I had made up my mind.

I stood in front of the big change-room mirror and applied a tiny bit of mascara, some blush, and lip gloss. Marla sat on the floor below me, curling her hair. After a little smack of my lips, I fluffed my hair one last time.

"What's with you?" Marla asked, making eye contact with me through the mirror, her eyes twinkling as if she was in on a big, juicy secret.

"Nothin'."

She winked at me. "You guys look good together."

"Yup." I winked back. "And he's coming for pizza with us." I grabbed my coat and bag. "Meet everyone there!" I called out.

Jonathon was leaning against the wall when I came out of the change room, and talking on his phone. When he saw me approach, he held up one finger. "I gotta go, Mom. Allie's here."

He nodded and pulled the phone away from his ear. "She says hi."

"Hi, back," I said, smiling. I wished I had a mother like her. Honestly, she was like the mothers on television shows, the ones who baked cookies and took their daughters shopping. My mother made me do the grocery shopping alone. Her idea of a mother-daughter shopping experience.

"Allie says hi back. Mom, I gotta go."

Obviously she kept talking because he didn't hang up right away. He nodded again and rolled his eyes. After a few more seconds, he said, "Love you too."

He pressed END and said, "She's so hard to get off the phone. She asks fifty questions about nothing."

I bumped my shoulder into his. "You're lucky."

His face broke out into this warm and oh-so-sexy smile, and he gently bumped me back. Shivers went from my head to my toes. Then he grabbed me by the waist and kissed me right in the hall.

A cough made us both straighten up and wipe our faces.

"Thought we were meeting you at the restaurant," said Marla, laughing behind her hand.

Ignoring the comment, I fell into step beside Marla and we all walked out together. Jonathon and I avoided holding hands or even touching.

"How's the rowing?" Marla asked him.

"Good," he answered. "I can't wait to get on the water, though. March can't come soon enough for me."

"I'm good friends with Mary on the women's rowing team," continued Marla. "She is so pumped to go to Victoria." We reached the front door and were hit with a blast of cold air when we stepped outside. Marla pulled her hood up and said, "I'm running."

Jonathon tossed his keys in the air. "My car or yours, Allie?"

"Do you have heat?"

"Uh, yeah. Don't you?"

"Nice try. Your car it is."

We didn't run but we did walk quickly to his Ford Escape. I rubbed my hands together when we got in, and he started the engine immediately. While it warmed up, he leaned over and touched my cheek. "I know how to get heat into your body," he whispered.

With bucket seats, I couldn't move right over to him, but I did stretch to be as close as I could.

He pressed his warm mouth to mine. I closed my eyes and let myself drift into our kiss. My body shook, but not because I was cold.

When we broke apart, he gazed into my eyes. "Are you warm now?" he whispered.

"Oh yeah," I whispered back.

He kissed the tip of my nose before he looked at his

temperature gauge. "Good to go." He flipped on the heat and backed out.

Conversation with Jonathon was easy, and we laughed a lot. I liked that nothing was forced and I didn't have to try to find things to talk about. Instead we talked music, bands, sports, even political stuff.

Most of the team was already at the restaurant when we arrived and I knew the girls were checking Jonathon out when we walked toward the table. Pride surged through me.

"Allie-bean!" called Marla. "Saved you a couple of seats."

The topic of conversation over dinner was, of course, Breanne's fight and Coach Cathy's technical foul. If Jonathon was bored, he sure didn't act like it. He joined in on the conversation and even talked to some of the other boyfriends even though they weren't all from Podium. Our noise level increased until our food arrived, then we all hunkered down to eat. Jonathon and I polished off a large pizza ourselves except for one piece. When we both grabbed it at the same time, our hands touched. We burst out laughing.

"I'll split it in two," I said coyly, meeting his eyes.

"But I've only had three pieces." He gave a comical frown. "That's not fair."

I shrugged playfully. "Nothing's fair." I turned away from him and split the piece in two, then handed him the bigger slice.

He leaned into me again and whispered in my ear, "You're amazing, you know."

I let my head fall against his shoulder. Forget my dumb family. I didn't need anyone else but him.

Jonathon drove me back to the school to pick up my car. While the engine warmed up, I waited in his. He touched my cheek with his finger and drew me close. Our lips locked and the kiss seemed to go on for a long time. My heart raced. My blood surged through me. When we broke apart, I was breathless, speechless, and wanted more, much more.

We kissed again and this time he put his hand on my thigh, inching it up. I opened my legs just a little to let his hand move higher. But then he pulled away, running his hand through his hair.

"Now's not the place or time," he said. "I want it to be right."

I kissed his cheek. "Me too," I said, my voice hoarse.

I got out of his car and ran to my beater. All the way home, I grinned, and I mean *grinned*. I cranked up my music and danced as I drove. When I got to the house and opened the garage, I saw both cars. I entered the house quietly, thinking my billets might be asleep. But the kitchen light was on and Abigail was standing by the fridge, getting a glass of water from the dispenser. She was dressed in her moss-green satin housecoat.

"Hi," I said. "How was dinner?"

"Great," she said, sipping her water. "That was quite a game."

"I know. Crazy, eh?"

"I've never seen girls fight in a basketball game before. Or in any game, for that matter."

I was about to reply that neither had I when John

walked into the kitchen, dressed in blue-and-grey flannel pyjamas. "Hi, Allie. Some game. That girl on your team is spirited. Sure she doesn't play hockey?" He strolled to the cupboard and got himself a glass. Once it was filled with water, he leaned casually against the kitchen counter, looking a bit like a geeky male model.

"Breanne was in shock," I said. "She said that when she got in the change room after the ref kicked her out, she sat still for like ten minutes."

"I think the crowd was equally shocked," said John. "Everyone went ballistic." He shook his head. "Even I stood up. That's a first."

"We could hardly hear the ref making the calls," I said.

"By the way," John said, nodding his head slowly, "that guy of yours is a good guy. We enjoyed sitting with him. He's got his act together."

"Yeah, he's really pleasant," said Abigail. "And smart. He'll go places." She downed her water and put her glass in the dishwasher. "I'd be hanging on to him." She yawned. "I'm going to bed."

"Me too," I said. "Thanks for coming to my game."

As I walked to my room, I thought, *Don't worry, Abigail, I will do everything in my power to hang on to him.*

CHAPTER EIGHT

"I don't want you to go." I ran my fingers up and down Jonathon's bare chest. We were in my bedroom, arms and legs tangled together. He still wore his jeans and I had a T-shirt on and pyjama shorts. Abigail and John were out of town for the night.

He kissed the top of my head and stroked my back. "I'm only gone for two weeks."

"Two weeks will seem like such a long time." I gazed up at him. "We've seen each other almost every single day since we started going out." All my basketball games in the past few weeks had been in Calgary or Edmonton or Red Deer, so I hadn't been away for long periods of time. And Jonathon was around all the time, except now he was leaving tomorrow to go to Victoria for two weeks.

"We can Skype." He nuzzled his nose into my hair.

His warm breath lit a fire in me that I just couldn't put out. He put his hand under my T-shirt and tenderly ran his fingers up and down my back. When he hit my bra strap, he carefully undid it. The unstrapping of my bra made me feel free and exposed in this really good way. My breasts longed to be touched. I moved slightly to allow his hands to wander. His hand cupped me, and everything I wanted to feel, I did. My breath came out in ragged gasps.

"Is that okay?" he said softly.

"Yes," I replied, closing my eyes. "I want the light off."

The click echoed off the walls.

We fooled around for a few more minutes, touching bare skin to skin. When he found this little place in my neck to kiss, my body trembled. I reached down and put my hands on the fly of his jeans. It was what I wanted. What I'd been fantasizing about. What I needed to do to keep him thinking about me while he was gone.

"You're okay with this?" he asked when we were naked.

"Yes," I answered.

He reached for his jeans, now on the floor, and then I heard the crinkling of a condom wrapper. I'm not sure what I was expecting, but it all seemed to happen quickly.

Then we lay in each other's arms under the covers, our breaths returning to normal. I could feel his heart beating and I laid my head on his chest. I closed my eyes and let my body mould into his. I guess if I was honest, I liked the before and after, liked just lying close to him better than the actual in-between. It stung a little down there, but it didn't hurt, really. But now I felt warm and cocooned because I was wrapped in his strong, muscled arms.

"Wow," he whispered, stroking my hair. "That was amazing."

"Yes," I replied in a whisper as I curled closer into his body.

Jonathon didn't stay the night because that would be pushing it. He had to be at the school to board the team bus at 8:00 a.m. Both the women's and the men's rowing teams were going on the training trip. So just before midnight, he dressed in the dark as I pulled on my pyjamas. Then I walked him to the door.

Our goodbye felt a bit strange; something had changed. He tenderly kissed me and I touched his cheek. Our gestures were simple.

After he left, I went back to bed, the place where we had just made love. I stared into the dark for a few minutes before I rolled over, curled into a ball, and tried to sleep. Sleep didn't come, though, and I couldn't turn my mind off. Did I feel different? *Was* I different? I put my hands between my legs and tried to think of Jonathon being in there, inside of me. Was it *everything* I thought it would be?

I felt so alone in my bed, in the house. Then it hit me. Even though I had Jonathon, I didn't have him. He wasn't with me now. Emptiness invaded me again and I wished it would just go away forever. Did I think having sex would take it away, take away all my problems, all my loneliness?

I woke the next morning and the first thing I did was pick up my phone. The time was 8:05. His bus had left, but he'd sent me a text at 7:30, which repeated what he'd said the night before: "last night was amazing."

At first I grinned, put my hand to my mouth, and giggled. I fell back on my bed and held the phone to my chest. It had actually happened.

Yes. Yes, it had.

I texted him back: "I can't stop thinking about us."

I waited to hear the familiar *ping* on my phone. Surely, after last night, he would send me another message right away. One minute went by. Two minutes. Three minutes. Soon ten minutes had passed. Why wasn't he texting back?

When he didn't, I sent him another one: "hope u have a safe trip"

Should I say that I missed him? No.

What was I going to do without him? *For two whole weeks.*

Basketball practice would help; it always did. Over the years it had been my escape. I looked at the time on my phone. I still had an hour before practice. I got up, went to my computer, and looked up "lobster chili." I had totally forgotten about this recipe.

I quickly sent it to his mother.

She immediately replied, saying thanks and she would give it a try, followed by a happy face. Her response made me smile and filled me with something warm.

I drove to the school, and at every stoplight, I glanced at my phone. His mother and I texted a few more times, but nothing came from Jonathon.

"What are you going to do without Jonathon for two weeks?" asked Marla as we headed across the gym floor to the trolley that held the balls.

"I'll live," I said with fake confidence. Then it hit me. Could she tell what had happened last night? Did I look different? To be honest, I did feel a bit different and I wasn't sure if it was all good. I had wanted to wait and now it was over, but the good thing was, Jonathon and I were a couple, so it hadn't just been sex to have sex. Should I tell Marla?

No, I had to tell Carrie first.

"My friend is in the female eight," said Marla, interrupting my thoughts. "She was so excited. She says they have a great time because the guys and girls just hang out together. They go on the water at the same time and eat at the same time. I think it would be fun."

I hadn't thought about *that*. I knew a few of the girls on the rowing team. Were any of them really good-looking?

"Which one is your friend?" I asked, trying to sound nonchalant.

"Mary. I'm not sure you know her. She's got long, blond hair and a killer bod."

Long, blond hair. I grabbed a ball off the cart. *Killer bod.* "Come on," I said. "Let's shoot hoops."

During practice we ran lines, and I worked up an amazing sweat. Physical exertion was exactly what I needed. We did a lot of pick-and-roll drills too, which required concentration. And a lot of offence, where I seemed to get loads of rebounds and was able to sink most off the backboard.

After practice, because it was Saturday, I decided to shower back at the house. Parm and I were getting together in the afternoon to work on math, and Carrie and I were getting together at night to watch movies and eat popcorn.

Keep busy, Allie. Keep busy. Time will fly by.

Walking to my car, I pulled out my phone and checked. Still no text. Why? What was wrong? Surely he could text me on the bus. It was a twelve-hour trip and he'd said he would.

I got back to the house, showered, and . . . moped. Big-time. In my room by myself. Two weeks would be forever if he was going to be a lazy texter. I mean, how many times had I checked today. A hundred? Crap. And it was only lunchtime. When I couldn't stand being with myself any longer, I went to the kitchen to make a sandwich.

I was slathering mustard on the bread when Abigail walked in the kitchen. "Hi," she said.

"Hi," I said back without looking at her.

"What's going on with you?" Abigail was like a closet psychologist.

"Nothing," I answered.

"I don't believe you," she said.

I turned to look at her and she genuinely looked interested in me and my foul mood. "Jonathon left today for two weeks," I said.

"Oh, I see," she nodded.

She totally surprised me when she said, "I understand how you feel. I remember when John and I first met and we spent all our time together. He went on a business trip and I missed him like crazy. But I dove into my work and time went by fast."

"That's what I'm going to do," I said.

She smiled. "You've got so much going on. Concentrate on your basketball. You're going places."

For a few seconds I couldn't say anything. Abigail rarely complimented me and never confided in me, and for the most part, I thought I annoyed her. Finally I said, "Thanks, Abigail. I really appreciate you saying that."

"You've been good for John and me. At first we weren't

sure about the billeting but it's been great."

I didn't step forward to hug Abigail, because she just wasn't the hugging kind, but deep down I knew we'd forged some new bond.

Parm showed up at exactly two because she was never late and never early.

"How was practice?" I asked.

"Hard. What about you?" The way she stared at me made me wonder if I had mustard on my face.

I refused to meet her penetrating gaze. "Our practice was hard too, although we did a lot of skills stuff, which I like."

"Allie, what's wrong?"

Holy. Could the entire world pick up on my moods? First Abigail, now Parm. It was like I was wearing one of those big mood rings that turned black when you were upset and green or blue or some colour when you were happy. Was I that transparent?

"Nothing's wrong," I said, lifting my chin. There was no way I could talk to Parm about Jonathon. She didn't need to know we'd had sex last night and that today he'd only texted me once. She'd tell me he was no good for me and I was going to get hurt, and I didn't want to hear that. "I'm just a bit tired."

"Oh, okay," she said.

We got down to work and, as usual, Parm the genius made me feel smart. I tried to be upbeat, to make her not think anything was wrong, but after I checked my phone for the millionth time, she put her pencil down. "What gives?"

"I'm just waiting for a text from Jonathon. I hope he made it okay."

She leaned back in her chair and relaxed and I figured we were taking a break.

"Oh right," she said. "The rowers are gone. I talked to my friend who's in the four-person boat. She was so pumped to go. She said it's the highlight of the year to go on these training sessions, even though they have to work their butts off. Her hands will be a mess of blisters when she comes back."

Immediately I thought of Jonathon's hands all over my body. Even though they were calloused, they were tender. I closed my eyes for a second.

Parm interrupted my thoughts. "There are not many teams who integrate the males and females like that. I guess they have a great time."

"Yeah," I said. "Jonathon says it's a blast." He hadn't said that. He hadn't really told me much about the fun stuff, just about the on-the-water training and the erg tests. Had he not told me for a reason? Was he trying to hide something from me?

I stood. "You hungry?" I walked to the fridge, opened it, and looked inside. "I could make us something." I searched the shelves, looking for anything that would take my mind off the thought of Jonathon having a great time without me.

"Do you miss him already?" Parm asked. Geez. Her brain wasn't only smart, it was intuitive.

"Not really." I kept looking in the fridge for food. "I could do a plate of cheese, crackers, pickles, and olives," I said.

"He hasn't even been gone a day," she said. "Usually you're so strong and independent."

I turned sharply. "I'm still the same person. Just because I have a boyfriend doesn't mean I've changed. And if I do miss him, so what? What's wrong with that?"

"Nathan, Donald, now Jonathon. I just hope you don't think these guys are a replacement for something." She closed her books and put her pencil away.

"Are you hungry or not?" I asked.

Parm's comment bothered me more than I wanted it to. It was early evening now and Jonathon had still not texted me. I couldn't stand not knowing where he was and what he was doing. Was he safe? Had the bus even got to Victoria? Was he on the ferry? Had I changed? Could sex for the first time change a person? Totally change their relationship?

I sent him another text before I left to go to Carrie's place. She lived with an older couple who were a lot less strict than Abigail about a mess, so it was better if we watched movies and ate popcorn at her place. On the way there, I picked up massive bags of licorice and plain M&Ms and at the last minute picked up a big box of Nerds. I didn't often indulge in junk food, but tonight I craved it.

I rang the doorbell at Carrie's and she yelled from behind the door, "Come on in!" I pushed the door open and walked in. Shoes were scattered in the front hallway and I smelled popcorn and heard popping.

"I'm in the kitchen!" Carrie shouted over the popcorn machine.

I slipped out of my shoes and headed to the kitchen.

"Look what I brought!" I held up the candy and waved it in the air.

The hot-air popcorn machine was going full tilt. "Red licorice! Awesome. Girl, we are going to have a good ol' girls' PJ party."

Suddenly the popcorn started to float out of the machine. And of course Carrie hadn't put the bowl close enough, so it started spilling all over the counter. I laughed and it felt good. I hadn't laughed all day.

Once the popcorn was ready, we took it and some big plastic glasses of ice water, as well as the candy, downstairs.

"Let's watch a chick flick." She put the food on the coffee table and picked up the remote.

We chose a movie with Kate Hudson and Ryan Reynolds and settled down to watch and eat. About ten minutes into the movie, when the romance wasn't quite working yet, Carrie looked at me and said, "How's Jonathon?"

"He left today." I chewed a piece of licorice.

"You miss him?"

I nodded. And just like that, tears welled behind my eyes and I turned my head. I still hadn't heard from him.

"Hey," she said softly, "it's okay to miss him."

"We had sex last night," I mumbled.

"What?!" Carrie grabbed the remote and put the movie on PAUSE. She stared at me. "What changed your mind? I thought you were going to wait until marriage."

"I dunno," I said. "It felt right."

Her face broke out in a huge grin. "I'm so glad you didn't wait. We need to celebrate! At least one of is going to graduate *not* a virgin." She tucked her legs up under her and said, "So tell me, tell me." She sang the words.

"He hasn't texted me all day." Tears spilled down my cheeks.

She gently touched my arm. "Hey, maybe the coaches took their phones. We always have to give our phones up when we're on the road."

"Oh my gawd! That's it." I slapped my forehead. "I bet that's why he didn't respond to my texts."

Carrie screwed up her face. "How many did you send?"

"Um, like ten." In all honesty, I had probably sent more than ten.

She swatted me. "All-ie. Guys hate that. And it's so not you."

"I couldn't help it. I was going insane not knowing where he was or who he was with. I don't get it. It's like the sex has changed our whole relationship. He's only been gone one day, and I miss him so much. I . . . I think I'm in love with him."

"You should be if you went all the way." Carrie tilted her head and smiled sweetly. "It's okay to love him." She reached over and hugged me before she held me by the shoulders. "Just don't lose yourself."

"I won't. I've watched my mom do it too many times."

"I'm so happy for you."

"One day it will be your turn," I said. We leaned back again, got totally comfy, and she turned the movie back on so we could watch Kate Hudson fall head over heels in love with Ryan Reynolds.

CHAPTER NINE

Carrie was right. Jonathon did have to turn his phone in to the coach for the bus ride and ferry ride. Why I had freaked was stupid. I should have just looked at the situation logically, but it seemed I wasn't looking at too much with a clear head when it came to Jonathon. From what he told me, they had done team-building exercises all the way to Victoria and they were given their phones back in the evening. He'd texted me right away, as soon as he got his phone, and thankfully he didn't mention all my texts. I told him I'd been worried so he wouldn't think I was this loser, stalker girlfriend.

From all his texts, though, I did sense he was having a good time. Yes, I wanted him to have a good time but not too good a time. Not without me.

Sunday dragged by. And I didn't send any texts even though I wanted to. I only texted him if he texted me, which was only once. I must have picked up my phone a million times.

Monday morning arrived and I couldn't wait to get to school. Classes, practice; my day would be busy and I needed that big-time. I met up with Carrie in the front lobby of the school.

"When's your next game?" she asked.

"Friday. We play this really good team from the States. Another home game. I wish we were on the road, because it would kill more time." I looked at Carrie. "You're gone, right?"

We turned at the end of the hall and headed up the stairs. "Yuppers," she said. "Big competition in Saskatoon."

For some reason, stairs always bugged my knee. "I think one of the girls on my team is having a party on Saturday," I said.

"Yeah, I heard," said Carrie. "I'd go if I was in town."

We reached the top and I gave my knee a quick rub before I slipped my arm through hers. "Thanks for listening yesterday. I must have sounded like a real whiner."

"Nah," said Carrie, "you didn't. This whole grade twelve thing and being done high school is all a bit confusing. Then if you throw in a guy *and* sex, I mean, your head must be ready to blow up."

I laughed. "I'm okay. Hey, you got a grad date yet?"

She shrugged. "There's always Jax. He was my boyfriend and now he's a buddy." She looked at me and I could see that something was going on with her.

"What's up?"

"At least you know what you're doing next year," she said. "Duke is an amazing school and you've got a full ride."

"Yeah, I'm lucky that way," I said. "No matter what happens with my dumb family, I can get away from them and play basketball. I bet Jonathon and I stay together through it all too. We can make plans for Thanksgiving and Christmas. You any closer to figuring out next year?"

"I still want to go to Vegas."

"You will. We'll both reach our dreams!" I bumped her with my hip.

She shrieked as only Carrie can and pretended to fall into the lockers.

"Girls," said Mr. Carruthers, who was walking down the hall on the other side. "Get to class."

Coach Cathy called me in for a meeting before practice. I had last block off and was just going to study in the library, so the timing was perfect. When I went in her office, I eased into the chair in front of her desk. Being named captain meant I had a lot of meetings with the coach.

"I want to talk to you about Jacquie," she said. "We have a big game this weekend against a really tough team, and Breanne is still out."

"Yeah, I've thought about that," I said.

"You're going to need to take her under your wing. Guide her. Perhaps you can work with her a bit this week. During practice be positive to give her confidence, but don't baby her. She needs to be up to speed by Friday night."

"No problem," I said. Coach Cathy never babied and I liked that about her.

She smiled. "I can always count on you." She paused. "I've been thinking." She casually leaned forward and interlaced her fingers. "I run a lot of camps in the summer.

I know you like to head home for the summer, but would you ever be interested in helping with some of them?"

"Like a summer job?" I asked.

"Yes, a summer job. Just from July 15 to August 15. I have one camp here in Calgary and then the rest are in Victoria and up the island."

"Wow," I said. I quickly gathered my thoughts. Jonathon would be in Victoria training, so I could see him more. This could be perfect, plus I wouldn't have to go home and be with my mother and her new boyfriend. "I'd be totally interested," I said.

"Good. We can discuss it further later. The camps don't start until that second week in July, so you could go home for a few weeks right after graduation. You can stay with me once the camps start, but I'll be away for those first two weeks of July. I also know your coach at Duke will want you there well before school starts, so I can be flexible on your end date."

"Okay," I said. Little did she know, I didn't want to go home after graduation. Perhaps I could stay with Abigail and John for a few extra weeks. Why not? They liked having me. This might be the perfect excuse not to go home. And, I was anticipating leaving early for Duke. Perhaps I didn't have to go home at all.

Coach Cathy stood up. "But, Allie, let me know if you want to spend summer at home in Halifax. I know how hard it is to be away all year and all summer too."

"It'll be fine," I said. "I'd love to teach at your camps. Sounds perfect."

"Talk to your mom, okay? She may want you home."

I stood tall. "She'll be okay with it." I looked Coach Cathy in the eye. "She only wants what's best for me." What a fat crock of crap that was.

I left Coach Cathy's office with a spring in my step. How lucky was that? I wouldn't have to go home in the summer and meet *Mike*. It would save my mother money, and that was more important to her than me coming home. And maybe she would realize how much I did for the family and Kat would realize what a big job it was to cook and clean. Plus, the best part was that Jonathon was from Victoria. I could go over to his house for dinner and his mother and I could cook together. Maybe we could even go to lunch if I had a day off.

The first drill we did in practice was an offensive drill. Before it started I ran over to Jacquie. "You have great ball-handling skills. Don't be afraid to shoot. I'll be there for the rebound. I promise. That's my job."

"Okay," she nodded. I could tell she was nervous.

When the drill started, we all had this crazy buzz going, and boy, did we move the ball around.

"Pass, pass, pass!" Coach Cathy yelled. "Faster. Faster!"

I knew she was trying to get Jacquie up to our speed. The first round, she fumbled and the ball went out of play. Coach Cathy drilled another one at her and she caught it and passed to Marla.

"Good job!" I hollered. "Let's keep it going."

We kept circling the ball around, and within a few minutes, Jacquie was catching and throwing with speed and accuracy.

"Okay, let's add some defence in there!" Coach Cathy blew her whistle and the second string — who were doing the same drill at the other end of the gym with our assistant coach — ran to our end. Breanne was with them and led the charge.

By the end of practice I was a bucket of sweat but felt great about the progress. Time had flown by and Friday night's game was at the front of my mind.

In the change room, I flopped down on the bench and wiped my face and neck with my towel. "Great practice," I said.

Marla sat down beside me. "I'll say. I'm looking forward to Friday. We have a pretty tough team to play on Saturday too."

"Bring it on." We slapped hands.

I yanked my phone out of my bag. Jonathon had sent me one text and had attached a photo of an empty boat on Elk Lake, a picturesque shot of calm water with no people. I preferred people shots.

"look at that glass. might have time to skype tonight"

The photo was maybe a bit lame, but the talk about Skyping wasn't. Beside me on the bench, Marla burst out laughing. "Too funny." She handed me her phone. "Look at the rowing team. They're like stupid crazy."

I took her phone and stared at the photo. All the guys and girls were planking all over a hotel room and it did look hilarious. They were across tables, beds, night tables, and each other, like stacked on top of each other.

Marla leaned into me and pointed to her screen. "There's Mary. Jonathon's on top of her."

My breath caught in my chest. Jonathon *was* on top of Mary, like lying right on top of her. I didn't want him on top of her. She wore shorts and a T-shirt, not sweatpants and a hoodie like the rest of the rowers. My heart rate picked up. His nose seemed to be imbedded in her *long, blond hair* and his body attached like glue to her *killer bod.* Why did he pick her to plank with? I wanted to laugh, say something funny, make it look like I didn't care, but no words or sounds came out.

Finally I coughed and handed Marla her phone. "That's sooo funny."

"You want to see the rest of the photos?" She started scrolling through, and even though I wanted to get up and go to the shower, I made myself look at them. In every photo, Jonathon was with Mary, and sometimes she was hanging on to him. What was with *that?*

"Who posted all these?" I asked.

"Mary. She loves to have a good time." Marla tossed her phone in her bag and stood. "I gotta get showered. I have so much homework tonight I could scream."

"Me too," I said, thinking about the screaming part. But my screaming wouldn't be because of homework.

At 7:00 p.m., just after I'd eaten a huge plate of chicken and quinoa, I went to my room, shut my door tightly, and flicked on my computer. I logged on to Skype. One minute later, Jonathon's smiling face showed up on my computer screen and I grinned.

"Hey, it's so good to see your face. How are you?" I asked, still smiling.

"Awesome." He blew me a kiss. "I miss you."

"I miss you too." I blew him a kiss back. "So much. How are your workouts?"

"Amazing. You saw that photo of the water this morning. It's great to be back in a boat."

"Yeah, it looked pretty."

We talked back and forth for about ten minutes. He never mentioned the planking and I didn't mention it either. Then I heard background noises, people talking.

"I should go," he said. "We have a team meeting."

"Is that some of the guys now?" I asked.

He turned his head away from the computer to look behind him. When he turned back, he had a huge grin on his face. "No, it's just crazy Mary."

She jumped into view and said, "Hiya, Allie."

I barely knew Mary, so why was she even saying my name or jumping in front of the computer to say hi to me? "Hi," I said back. "I should let you go," I said to Jonathon.

"Yeah, okay." He burst out laughing. "Hey, don't do that." He obviously was talking to Mary and not me. "That tickles." He turned back to me and said, "I gotta go."

"Yeah, me too," I snapped.

I turned off my computer, gritting my teeth. Could it be any more obvious that she was flirting with him? And he was so far away and I could do nothing about it. I picked up my phone and fired off a text:

"miss u, can't wait to see u"

I was about to toss my phone on my nightstand when it rang. I glanced at the number and saw it was Kat.

"Hey Kat."

"How's it, uh, going?" she asked. "You sound kinda weird."

"I'm okay." There was no way I wanted her to know I was pissed off because some girl was flirting with my boyfriend. And that I'd had sex. Kat would be disappointed in me. Ever since Mom had turned into a total slut last summer, Kat and I had decided we wanted to wait. I had to make myself sound more upbeat. "How about you? What's going on?"

"It seems like forever since you've been home," she said. "But everything's pretty good around here. Mom, she's happy with Mike."

I rolled my eyes even though I was alone in my room. "Next thing you know he'll be moving in."

"She got her divorce from Dad yesterday," Kat said quietly.

"They're really divorced?"

"I think they both wanted to be free."

"What, so they both can remarry again, within like seconds, and make the same mistakes they did the first time round?"

"She said she tried to call you."

"I've been busy."

Kat didn't respond for a few seconds. I could hear her breathing. Finally she said, "Are you going to work at the Bistro again this summer?"

"I dunno. Why? Summer is still months away." After I'd told Coach Cathy I'd work for her, I'd lain awake wondering how I would tell Kat. I still hadn't worked up the nerve and now here she was asking me about my old job.

Again a pause from Kat. She had something to tell me so I just let the silence happen. Finally she said, "I think I want to work there this summer."

I sat up. "I thought you had a job at a coffee shop."

"The Bistro would be better money."

Something bothered me about this and I blurted out, "Are you trying to take over my life?"

I wasn't sure why I was so bugged that she wanted to work at the Bistro when I wasn't even coming home. But I was. Did they not want me to come home?

"I suppose you're cooking and cleaning now too," I said.

"Mom's been cooking a lot. She made that chili the other day. You remember the one we loved when we were little? I still do some cooking, though."

Was Kat telling the truth? Mom hadn't cooked in years. "Well, don't take over for her."

"Allie, it's okay. I don't mind helping her if she's working. And I'm good at it. Mike thinks I'm a great cook."

Mike this, Mike that.

"Well, if that's the case, maybe I won't come home," I snapped. My heart pounded like I'd just run the length of the gym. My family was trying to dump me.

"I'm sorry," she said. "I don't have to work at the Bistro."

"Go ahead. I don't care where you work. Anyway, I've got a job teaching at camps for my coach all summer. In Calgary and Victoria."

"That's great, Allie."

"Maybe I'll never come home again. Ever. Then I won't have to meet Mike."

"Allie, you have to come home."

"Why?"

There was silence on the other end and it hung in the air like the smell of dirty socks. "Spill, Kat."

"Okay, but promise me you won't say I told you."

"I promise," I muttered.

"No, like you mean it."

"Okay, okay. I promise."

"Mike is gonna ask Mom to marry him."

"I can't deal with this," I said. "I have to go."

When I hung up the phone, I was convinced I was making the right decision not to go home. The woman had just got divorced. Why did she want to get married again? I didn't want anything to do with this wedding. I had everything I needed for university. I could fly from Calgary to Duke, buy my own plane ticket with the money I made teaching at the camps. My mother didn't help me move in here when I first came to Podium in *grade ten*. I'd flown out on my own and fended for myself.

Jonathon and his family were more like my home and I'd only met them once. How crazy was that? Maybe instead of asking Abigail if I could stay with her and John, I could go to Victoria with Jonathon. That was a much better idea and I wondered why I hadn't thought of it earlier. A road trip to Victoria would be a blast. We would laugh the whole way and buy junk food at gas stations. I had a plan!

CHAPTER TEN

I made it through the week because of basketball. Friday rolled around and I was jacked to play and wanted nothing more than to win. Jacquie had really being pulling her weight, and as a team, we had confidence in her.

I showed up at the gym early, which was typical of me. Being alone in the gym before a game was my ritual. It was my time to visualize my game: jumping, shooting, and swishing the ball through the net.

How long I sat there before I heard a noise, I had no idea. The sound of shoes squeaking on the waxed floor made me look to the door. Jacquie came toward me.

"Hey," I said.

"I hope I'm not interrupting," she said.

"No. I'm just getting ready to play," I said. "You want to warm up together?"

"Sure," she answered.

I looked at her and smiled. "You'll do great tonight."

"I hope so."

"You know so. Come on, let's shoot."

We passed the ball back and forth and Jacquie moved

quickly and solidly, her hands and feet moving rhythmically. I kept readjusting my brace. After about fifteen minutes, some of our other teammates showed up.

I stopped moving and put the ball under my arm. "Let's get dressed for the game," I said to Jacquie.

"I'll put the ball away," she said.

I threw it to her and it was then I saw Parm standing at the back door of the gym with this strange look on her face. And she was staring at Jacquie, not me. Weird. *Was she jealous of Jacquie too?* I didn't wave to her because that wasn't something I did before I played. I needed to focus, prepare, and make sure I took some pain relievers

The game started and we were flying up and down the court. I had this insane energy zinging through my body and I jumped higher and ran faster and played with an intensity that usually came to me when I was in a playoff game or at Parents Weekend. At halftime the score was 24–20 for us. I downed two more pain relievers.

At the jump ball to start the second half, I got the ball to Jacquie. She started dribbling, taking control, and glancing around to see who she could pass to. Her hesitation and uncertainty showed, and when she made a long pass to Lydia, I saw the opposing player running to intercept the ball. She succeeded and headed toward our zone. I screeched to a halt and my knee buckled, but I ran back anyway. The player from the other team was fast and she sank the ball.

I said to Jacquie, "It's okay."

Jacquie nodded, but the confidence she'd shown in the first half seemed to be waning. Next play she had the ball and we were in their zone, hoping for a basket. She passed to me. I immediately fired a pass back. My throw was hard and she fumbled the ball. She tried to pick it up but it rolled out of bounds. The ref made the call and we lost possession.

We ran back to play defence, and their guard brought it up and sank a three-pointer. We were now trailing by a point. Coach Cathy yelled at Jacquie from the sidelines and I ran down with her.

"Be ready," I said. Enough of the babying. She had to suck it up or get subbed out.

Jacquie made a few good plays and seemed to settle down. She got the ball to Lydia, who took a shot. I flew in for the rebound, but the ball hit the backboard on a weird angle and bounced up and over. Again we took off down the court.

The same sharpshooter moved forward on us. Jacquie made a lunge at her and tripped her. The ref blew his whistle. Foul. We lined up on the key and the girl sank both her shots. Finally we had possession again.

"Karen," I yelled, "take it down!"

I could see Jacquie's face drop but I didn't care. We were losing.

At the break between the third and fourth quarter, I looked at Coach Cathy. Was she going to take Jacquie out of the game? To throw someone else in from the bench this late in the game, playing against such a strong team, would not do us any good.

The ref blew his whistle and we took to the floor. On the way over I patted Jacquie on the back. "Play *your* game, not theirs."

I squatted low on the jump ball, determined to win it,

and when I jumped, I got great height and sent it back to Lydia. When I landed, though, a sharp jab of pain shot through my knee. *Not now,* I thought. I gritted my teeth and ran forward to give Lydia someone to pass to.

One quarter left. You can do it. Mind over matter.

Although we tried and played better in the fourth quarter than we did in the third, we ended up losing the game by two points.

"Good effort," said Coach Cathy. "They are a good team. Can we beat them? Yes. Did we? No. We lost our momentum in the third quarter and let them in. With a team like this, that can't happen. It's a lesson. We meet them again this season and next time we'll be better prepared."

I picked up my towel and heard Marla grumbling about Breanne not being there and if she had been we wouldn't have lost. I glanced at Jacquie and saw the crestfallen look on her face and knew she had overheard Marla. Sport was tough on the ego.

"Hey," I said to her. "It's one game. You played great for three quarters."

She hung her head. "Coach Cathy is so mad at me. So are the girls."

"Don't go there," I said. "Chin up and move on, but learn from your mistakes. And Coach Cathy is like that. She'll cool down."

She slowly lifted her gaze to meet mine. "Thanks," she said.

I slung my arm around her. "Toughen up, girl, and you'll be a starting guard next year."

In the change room Marla stood on the bench and

yelled, "I hope everyone is coming to my party tomorrow right after the game." She moved her shoulders as if she was dancing.

"We just lost," I barked. "Can we talk about the party later?" I iced my knee, shaking my head. I hated losing. The change room fell silent.

Music blared from the iPod docker and Marla's parents were nowhere in sight when I walked through her front door. She was one of several athletes at Podium whose families lived in Calgary. Most thought living at home was a luxury, but not me. I'd rather billet than live with my mother and her soon-to-be-*fiancé* who, according to my little sister Olive, was now sleeping over all the time and using the spare room as his personal closet. It just so happened that the spare room was where I had my extra clothes. Suits, shirts, men's boring shoes were now all mingled in with the clothes I'd left behind.

Gag me.

"Allie, you came!" Marla shouted over the music.

"Of course," I replied. I glanced around the room and saw a bunch of boys I didn't know. Marla leaned into me. "My little brother invited a few friends. I had to let him so he wouldn't tell our parents. If you see him drinking, tell me, okay? He promised he wouldn't, but he's a little turd."

I nodded. "Sure thing." Marla left me to go talk to someone else and I made my way to the kitchen. I had driven over, so I wasn't going to drink, plus I'd only ever been drunk once in my life, a night that had turned out to be a huge disaster. It wasn't my thing. Besides, I'd taken painkillers to get through the game, and it didn't take a genius to know that pills and alcohol didn't mix.

"Al-lie!" Lydia waved to me from across the room. Right away, I noticed that she had a bit of a glow on. That surprised me because usually she didn't drink. With Breanne out, though, Lydia had been a star, so she was obviously in the mood to celebrate. I watched as she grabbed Karen's arm and the two of them stumbled over to me. Now Karen was a different story. She was known as the girl who could down beer like a guy. Guys loved her. We called her Kickass Karen.

"Have you seen Aaron from the hockey team?" Lydia asked, her words slurring a little.

"I just got here," I said. "Why're you asking?" I teased.

"She thinks he's cute!" Karen squealed.

"I thought he was going out with a girl from the volleyball team," I said. "That's the last I heard."

Lydia looked pouty. "I think he still likes Carrie," she said.

Karen hiccupped, then laughed. "Podium is like the soap opera my brother watches every day." She was really slurring her words. "Do you think Kade likes Jacquie? I think Kade's cute."

"Nooo," wailed Lydia. "I heard a rumour Jacquie's into girls. Like Parm. And I heard another rumour that Parm has a thing for you, Allie." She playfully poked me with her finger.

"Not a chance," I said. "She's one of my best friends."

"Yeah, you're right. She's too sensible. I just love her no-nonsense approach to life." Lydia turned to Karen. "Your brother watches soap operas? That's crazy." Lydia burst out laughing.

"Yeah, isn't it sooo dumb. My other brother and I tease him mer-ci-less-ly." She giggled. "Wow, that was a huuuge mouthful."

I wondered if she liked to party because it made her forget about her mother dying.

"But seriously," Karen continued, wagging her finger, "everyone goes out with everyone on the soap operas and they marry each other like a gazillion times. It's kinda like Podium, well not the marrying, but look at you Allie. You were with Jonathon, and now he's with that Mary chick-eroo."

"He's not with Mary," I said. "We're still together. He's just away."

"Yeah," said Lydia laughing and pushing Karen, who toppled into the wall. "He's still with Allie. They're like a perfect couple."

Karen looked at me, but her eyes were really droopy. "Then you must be sooo pissed off with all that chick's stupid Facebook posts. I mean, she is all over him. I'd be kickassing her to friggin' China."

"I'm gonna get a drink of water," I said.

I didn't stay long at the party because I couldn't think straight or act happy. Fortunately Abigail and John weren't home when I got back to the house, steaming mad. I headed straight to my room and my computer. Before even taking off my coat, I logged on and went directly to Mary's Face-book page. Even though we weren't friends, I was able to look at all her photos. Of course, she didn't have them on privacy settings. Because, of course, she wanted the world to see the eighty million photos she posted every day.

I scrolled through her album labelled "Victoria," and sure enough, she was with Jonathon in every shot. Could he not say no to her?

After looking at the photos, I picked up my phone and texted him:

"hey let's skype"

I looked at more photos as I waited for him to answer, and with every one, my blood raced a little faster. My phone pinged.

"how was ur game?"

That was his text? He didn't say anything about Skyping. What was with that? I wanted to Skype. Know that he was in his room without her.

"good can u skype?"

"not now maybe later"

"u with Mary?"

I pressed SEND. Immediately I felt sick. Why did I say that? Stupid. Stupid. Stupid. Texts and emails were sometimes dangerous; it was too easy to just press SEND. My phone pinged again.

"no. why?"

Was I taking this too far? No. Karen had said something. Everyone must be talking about me behind my back. How could he do this to me? We had sex, then he went away and had begun flirting with fun, adorable, photo-snapping Mary.

"u r always with her"

"she knows u r my girlfriend. trust me."

Did I trust him? After my mother's idiotic choices, I don't think I trusted very many people.

CHAPTER ELEVEN

"So I think I've got a summer job," I said to Jonathon.

"Oh yeah." He speared a chicken wing and put it on his plate. Red hot sauce dripped onto the table in the transfer. He'd been home for over a week and this was our first chance to spend some time together. He'd wanted to go to an action movie, but I wanted to talk, so we'd gone to wing night at a pizza joint.

He gnawed on his wing. Obviously the twenty-five-cent wings were more important than my summer job. He'd come home and everything had been great for a few days, but I couldn't get the stupid Mary photos out of my mind. Then I saw them talking by his locker.

"My coach asked me to teach at her basketball camps, and some of them will be in Victoria," I said.

He wiped hot sauce off his mouth and glanced at me. "Cool," he said. He took a sip of water. "These are so hot. Amazing." He stabbed another wing. "When will you be in Vic?"

"End of July. We're there for two weeks. We could get together."

"Bummer," he said. "I'll be at the Henley Regatta in Ontario."

"Oh." I slouched in my seat. "Maybe I can visit your parents."

He looked at me with this puzzled expression. "That might be kind of awkward if I'm not there. You've only met them once."

I shrugged. "They were nice. And sometimes your mom and I text."

"You do? About what?"

"Recipes and stuff."

He did this weird thing with his eyebrows as if to say, *Really.* "Um, I guess you could try to get together, but they spend the summer in Kelowna."

"Will you be there the first two weeks of July?" All week I had been working up the courage to ask him if I could go home with him at the end of the school year. Just for two weeks. I wanted to put my plan of a road trip into action.

"Should be." He sat back and touched his stomach. "I'm stuffed."

"Aren't you going to ask why I asked about July?"

"I've got to finish my school year before I start thinking about July." He groaned.

I sucked in a deep breath before I said, "Can I stay with you and your parents those first two weeks of July?" The words spewed from my mouth.

"You mean in Victoria?" He squished his eyebrows together.

I nodded. "I don't want to go home."

"Why? Everyone wants to go home for a bit."

"It's complicated," I said. I searched his face to see if I could figure out what he was thinking. I wanted him to be excited to possibly spend two weeks with me. "And it's far," I added.

"It's my peak training time," he said. "We row in the morning and the evening and I nap in the afternoon. I wouldn't have much time to see you."

Don't cry. Don't cry.

I inhaled and looked down at my plate, piled high with bones. They started to blur in front of me and I knew the tears were there, creating a film over my eyes. I felt his hand on top of mine.

"Allie," he said softly, "what's wrong?"

I looked up and met his eyes, and right away I saw that he really was confused. "What's wrong?" I bit my bottom lip to stop the tears. "I ask if I can stay with you and you tell me you'll be too busy."

"But I will be," he said. "That's the truth." He paused but only for a second to tilt his head. "You're an athlete so I thought you would understand. It's not that I don't want to spend the time with you, it's that I *can't*."

"Forget I asked." I turned my head.

"Allie, summer is my season. I have to spend it with my team."

"And *Mary*." As soon as I said her name, I wished I hadn't.

He immediately withdrew his hand. "Not this again." He shook his head. "I've told you, I have nothing going on with her." He picked up the bill the waiter had dropped off and pulled out a twenty. "I think we should go."

All the way home in his car, I stared straight ahead. When he parked in front of Abigail and John's, he didn't turn the ignition off.

"Do you want to come in?" I asked. "It's early."

"Why? So you can grill me about something I never did?"

"I'm sorry," I said.

"You realize you've said that, oh, about a hundred times since I've been home. It's only been a week." His sarcastic tone made me look at him and that's when I saw the hurt in his eyes.

I reached over and took his hand in mine. "Have you thought about what we'll do next year?"

"Yes. Of course I have." He lifted my hand, kissed the back of it, and placed it in my lap. Then he leaned back and stared at the roof of his car. "And to tell you the truth, I'm not sure I can deal with a long-distance relationship." He rolled his head and glanced at me. "I went away for two weeks and you didn't trust me for a minute. We're going to be apart ninety percent of the time."

"She was hanging all over you," I said in defence.

"And I did nothing in return because I had a girlfriend." He sat up. "I can't keep defending myself to you, and it will be way worse when we're at university." He paused. "So, what's the real reason you don't want to go to Halifax?"

"I want to teach at the camp," I said, avoiding the truth.

"I get that. But you said it doesn't start until the middle of July. Go home for those first few weeks. I'm sure if your coach really wants you to teach, she'll pay for your flight back."

"I wanted to be with you," I said.

"I think there's more to it than that. Allie, talk to me."

"There's nothing more!" I snapped. "I wanted to spend time with you and I thought this was a good way."

He ran his hand through his hair and gave an exasperated sigh.

"I better go in," I said.

"Yeah, you better," he replied.

Our kiss goodbye was a hurried peck, even though we had tons of time.

"What is going on with you and Jonathon?" Carrie asked as we walked down the hall on Friday morning. I was only attending my morning classes, as my team was leaving for Edmonton at noon.

"We're fighting," I answered.

"Why? You guys are perfect."

"I asked him if I could stay with him for the first two weeks of July and he said he wouldn't have time to see me." I shifted my books to hold them across my chest as if they might protect my heart.

"Because of rowing?" Carrie asked.

I nodded.

"Allie, that's a reason."

I blew out a breath. "I know, I know. And then there's this Mary stuff."

"OMG, girl." Carrie stopped walking and spun me around to face her. "He doesn't like her. He likes *you*. He had sex with *you*."

I started walking. "I wish we'd never had sex. It changed everything."

"No. It changed *you*. You became the clingy girlfriend. Anyway, I heard Mary's going out with some university guy. She's having a big party this weekend. Should be fun."

"A party!" I looked at Carrie like she had two heads. "Jonathon didn't say anything to me about going to a party."

"Probably 'cause he knew you'd freak. Relax, Allie. The guy is like committed to you."

I blew out another breath, making my lips vibrate. All week I had been crabby with Jonathon, asking about his every move. I even went so far as to check his phone to see if she'd texted him. I wasn't going to tell Carrie *that*. She would probably yell at me in the hall and then everyone would know I was one of *those* girlfriends.

"I just can't seem to stop myself from overreacting," I said. "Now he's going to a party while I'm gone? The thought makes me nuts."

"Why're you being so weird about all of this?" Carrie asked.

"I dunno." I paused before I said, "Here's the truth. It's like he's too good for me. What if he finds out about my family?"

We came to our classroom door and stood outside because we had two minutes before class started.

"I honestly don't think he'd care," said Carrie, shifting her books onto her hip. "Except that you lied to him. I know you don't want to go home this summer, so why don't you ask Abigail if you can stay with them for the two weeks?"

"I did. She and John are busy and she said her contract with the school is up when the school year is over."

"She said that? What a bitch."

"Who's a bitch?" Parmita had somehow snuck up on us and butted into our conversation.

"Allie's billet," said Carrie. "She asked if she could stay for two weeks in July and Abigail said no."

Parmita shrugged. "Abigail's OCD. What'd you expect?"

"A little *sympathy from you* would be nice," I said to Parmita. Usually I could count on Parm to take my side.

"I'm sorry," she said, sounding sincere. Then she asked quietly, "Did you and Jonathon break up?"

"No. We didn't." I turned and stalked into the classroom, finding a seat at the back of the room.

Jonathon and I met to say goodbye after second class. "I'm sure you'll have a great weekend," he said. Did I detect a sound of relief in his voice or . . . was I imagining things? My head was bursting because it was like I had to decipher every one of his words.

"I'm sure you will too," I said.

"Yeah. I've got so much homework."

And a party to go to. Why wasn't he telling me about the party? Did he think he had to keep it a secret from me?

"You going out at all?" Yes, I was prying, but it was better than letting him know I knew he was going to a party at *Mary's.* I didn't dare mention her name again.

He shrugged. "Not sure yet. See what transpires."

He leaned into me and tried to kiss me. For some stupid reason, I pushed him away. I couldn't help myself, but at the same time, I hated myself for doing it. I really wanted to kiss him.

"What's wrong now?" he asked, sounding exasperated with me. *Again.*

"I know about the party," I stated.

"For shit's sake, Allie, grow up. I wasn't going to go to the party because I knew it would make you mad. But you know what? I'm going now."

He sucked in a big breath and closed his eyes. I knew he was gathering his thoughts. My body started to shake. What had I done?

When he opened his eyes, he said softly, "I hope you have a good weekend. And I mean that. But honestly I can't take any more. This is not how I wanted it to happen and the timing stinks, but I think we both need to have a break or something. All we do is fight."

I watched him walk away and a huge lump formed in my throat.

CHAPTER TWELVE

I boarded the bus, found a row in the middle, and put my bag on the seat beside me so no one would sit with me. I didn't want idle chatter. With everything else in my life falling apart, I had to focus on my basketball.

As I looked out the window at the dull grey sky, I couldn't believe Jonathon and I had *maybe* broken up. Had we? Was it true? My mood matched the sky. Perhaps he was just overreacting, like I had been overreacting. We could talk and get back together.

Voices sounded all around me. Happy voices. Athletes excited by a road trip. Jonathon was right, the timing was horrible. If I hadn't said something about the party, would he have just broken up with me anyway, after my weekend? Or would we have stayed together?

So confusing. But no matter what, I couldn't let this hurt my game or take down my team. Even though I was stuck on a bus, I had to try to be upbeat and positive.

I was the captain.

I ran my finger along the glass of the window, watching the little drops of condensation trickle down. Yes, I was confused and angry at myself for ruining something good, but I wouldn't cry until I was alone. Maybe he would miss me, and after the road trip we would get back together. I put my pillow behind my head and closed my eyes, hoping sleep would fix everything.

I awoke before we got to Edmonton and Coach Cathy told us our roommates. I was with Marla. That I could handle; if she asked too many questions, I could just tell her to stop.

I managed to get through check-in at the hotel and the team meal. No one asked me if I was okay or what was wrong, so I must have put on a pretty good face.

When we got to the gymnasium at the University of Alberta — we were playing the U of A Bears — I inhaled the smell of wood and wax and sweat. My world. This was mine no matter what else was happening around me. When I exhaled, I felt better, more relaxed, and ready to play. Breanne was back tonight and chances were she would be out for a personal best, especially after having to sit out for so long. Coach Cathy had informed us that the Bears team was tough; they were older and bigger. Tonight, nothing mattered more to me than basketball and winning.

After warm-up, I downed two pain relievers. They would get me through the quarter and maybe the half. I pushed all thoughts of Jonathon aside and took my position at centre for the jump ball, against a girl who was as tall as me but beefier. The ref threw it in the air and I exploded and ripped the ball from her hand, passing it back to Marla.

When I landed, my knee felt strong, so I took off down the court, hoping to get a pass or rebound and put us on the board. Marla threw the ball to Breanne and she faked a jump and passed back to Marla. The ball came to me and I passed to Karen, who sent it back to me. Around and around, our passes were crisp and clean. When I saw Breanne jump, I barrelled in for the rebound. As I was moving forward, I felt a knee on my knee and I tripped and crashed to the floor. The whistle blew. Foul.

It doesn't hurt. It doesn't hurt.

I lined up at the free-throw line and stared at the orange rim and white netting. I lined up the ball with the basket, bent both knees and took my shot. *Swoosh.*

One down.

Swoosh.

Both shots in.

At the half we were losing by one basket. I snuck in a couple more pain relievers before Coach Cathy gathered us around. "Great job, ladies. To be playing so aggressively with this team is what I want from you. Don't back down. Keep it up."

We took to the court again. I crouched super low, hoping to get as much height as I could. I jumped, reached, and fought for the ball. This time I lost, so I ran down the court. Playing defence, I watched the ball, anticipating the shooter's next move. When I saw her fake, I knew exactly where she was going and I lunged forward, snatched the ball out of mid-air and took off running.

Feet pounded behind me. When I was close to the basket, I took two long strides and leaped into the air. That's when I felt the hit. The opposing player had jumped with me and made body contact, knee against knee. I shot anyway, aiming for the backboard. As soon as the ball left my hand, I felt the entire force of her body against mine and I lurched sideways. With my body off balance, I landed on just one knee. My bad knee.

Pop. Pop. Pop.

I swear the noise of the rip echoed through the gym. Horrific pain shot through me and I fell to the floor, moaning, rolling around holding my knee. The ref blew his whistle and I just kept rolling and screaming. I couldn't help myself. I gasped for breath. Coach Cathy and our trainer, Melissa, ran across the floor to me.

"Can you get up?" Coach Cathy knelt beside me.

I tried to breathe, hoping to get rid of the stabbing pain. It drove through me like nails being hammered into my muscles. I kept gulping in air. More. More. It didn't do any good.

I tried to look at Coach Cathy but everything was spinning. The pain made me queasy and dizzy. Suddenly my knee went numb. I lay on the floor until a stretcher was brought and I was taken off the court. I heard the crowd clapping but it sounded tinny and far away. I was taken to the trainers' room at the university.

I was given some heavy-duty painkillers and then the university physio poked and prodded. Finally he said, "My guess is ligaments. You need an MRI right away and a good orthopaedic doctor."

Ligaments? I leaned back on the pillow and stared at the ceiling. Ligaments took forever to heal because of the limited blood flow to them. They were an athlete's curse.

"Cathy is looking into booking you an MRI," said Melissa.

"I don't have money for one," I muttered.

"She said either the school pays or she will. How does it feel?"

"Better. I'll be ready to play tomorrow. I know my knee and it's not ligaments."

But by the next night, I wasn't even close to being ready to play. I couldn't walk. Coach Cathy got me some crutches and painkillers with codeine. My emergency MRI was booked for Monday in Calgary and she was driving me. I was to ask no questions about the cost. It was being covered and that was all I needed to know. When she asked if my parents knew about my knee, I told her I'd talked to them.

I watched my team from the sidelines, and although my knee ached, my heart ached more. How could this have happened to me? Basketball was all I had. Especially now. I didn't text or phone anyone — not Carrie, Parm, Jonathon, or my parents like I'd told Coach Cathy. This injury could be like my last one, which had healed after a few days off. Maybe by Monday when I was back at school, the swelling would be down and everything would be okay. My knee had been through a lot and had always come through in the end.

Coach Cathy picked me up Monday morning at nine and my knee was still double the size. All night I'd tossed and turned, trying to get comfortable. I still hadn't talked to anyone. Coach Cathy had me scheduled for blood work, X-rays, and the MRI. We didn't talk much in the car on the way over to the medical clinic.

Finally she said, "You know if it is ligaments, you'll be out for a while."

"I refuse to believe it's ligaments," I said.

"Okay," she said, "fair enough. We'll wait for the results."

The blood work and X-rays were familiar tests, but I'd never had an MRI before. The procedure was explained to me and I had to lie still on my back in a long tubular thing that reminded me of a coffin. As it inched forward, I looked up at the sterile white ceiling of the tube and thought that if my knee was shot, I might as well be dead and in a coffin. For what would I have left? My family had given away my room and my mother was a train wreck. Jonathon, the only guy I'd had sex with, had broken up with me. All my friends at Podium would move on in their sports, become successful, make Vegas shows and national teams, and I would go nowhere. If I couldn't play basketball, then I didn't have a summer job and I might have to defer my first year at Duke and go home to a family who didn't care. Without basketball I had nothing.

Nothing. Nothing. The word chimed in my mind as I lay perfectly still, staring at nothing but blank white. My life would have zero meaning and I would have no reason to live. There was this huge part of me that would just want to die.

"I don't want to go to school today," I said on the way home with Coach Cathy.

"Okay. I can talk to your teachers."

"And I'm not going back until I hear the results."

"Do you think that's wise?" she asked. "You've always been someone who faces a problem head-on."

I rested my head against the cold glass of the window. "Not this time," I said. "Now there are too many problems."

CHAPTER THIRTEEN

After Coach Cathy dropped me off, I hobbled to my room. When my phone buzzed I ignored it. I flopped down on the bed, hoping that if I stayed in bed all day, maybe by night my pain would be gone and everything would be a bad dream.

I closed my eyes but didn't sleep. Time moved on without me. Hours later I heard Abigail come home. When she knocked on my door, I said, "What?"

She opened the door a crack. "How are you?"

"Okay," I answered.

Normally she would have left me alone, but tonight she walked right into my room. "I'm worried about you," she said. "The Allie I know would be showing some sort of emotion."

"Nope," I said in a bland voice.

"Would you like some dinner? I can bring it to your room."

That was a first, Abigail allowing food in my room. "Thanks," I said. "But I'm not very hungry."

"John and I have to go out in a bit. Do you think you'll be okay?"

"I'll be fine," I said.

Abigail shut my door and once again I was surrounded by the four walls and silence. I must have dozed off because when I opened my eyes, the room was dark.

White noise hummed in the background. But other than that, the house was quiet. Eerily quiet. I didn't move to turn on the lights. This horrible feeling of dread pressed on my chest, making it hard for me to breathe. I gasped and tried to take shallow breaths. My knee ached. My head ached. But most of all, my heart ached. Everything in my life seemed to be disintegrating, dissolving.

The dark encased me. Cold circled me. No light. I had no light in my life. Nothing. What if the MRI results said I couldn't play ever again? I didn't want to hear what the doctors said. I didn't want them to tell me something horrible. What if I slept through the appointment?

Or what if I just wasn't around to go to the appointment?

Would anyone miss me?

My parents didn't care about me anymore. Jonathon dumped me. Carrie was going to Vegas. Parmita would become a doctor.

"Everyone has their own life to live," I whispered, "but me."

Over the years I would be forgotten. I would become just another injured high school athlete. But in the end, who really cared? I wondered what would happen if I died. Would I go to a better place, be in heaven? Would people come to my funeral? I rolled my head and glanced at my nightstand.

That's when I saw the full bottle of painkillers with codeine. What would happen if I downed the entire bottle?
It would be easy. Painless. I'd just fall asleep and never
wake up. What would be the harm? Or maybe I wouldn't
die but just sleep for a really long time. I needed something to take away the painful throbbing in my chest, in
my heart. It pounded through my skin, my clothes, seemed
to reach every bone and muscle of my body. I just wanted
the pain to end.

I sat up and picked up the orange pill bottle.

I stared at it, rolling it around in my fingers. Around and
around. The movement mesmerized me. The pills clicked
against the side of the plastic. The noise had a weird rhythm.
Around and around. Visions of people flashed through my
mind.

I could see Kat crying, standing by a photo of me. Mom
had her arm around her. She was crying too. My mind
clicked to a huge auditorium filled with students and
teachers. Carrie was crying. Parmita too. And even Jonathon. Suddenly my mind went dark. Everything shifted
and I could see my family laughing at the beach, eating
lobster without me, and then the slide show went to an
auditorium with no people. No one showed up. No one
cared.

I popped open the lid on the bottle.

I heard a tapping noise in the distance, but ignored it. I
shook all the pills into the palm of my hand. I liked their
pretty blue colour. One mouthful. I could down them all
at once and lie back in my bed and just drift off. Maybe
when I woke up, everything would be okay and I could

play again and Jonathon would be my boyfriend and my mom would love me.

"Allie?"

I didn't answer the distant voice and instead just stared at the pills. Yes, they were pretty. Pale blue. Like the sky. Like heaven maybe. I wanted to be up there, in the sky.

"Allie!"

A bright light filled the room. I blinked. If I took them, would I go to the light? Hands shook my shoulders. The pills fell to the floor, scattered like little bugs.

"What are you doing?!"

Parm's voice jolted me back to reality. "I dunno," I answered. "I don't know what I'm doing."

And I didn't know. That was the truth.

I gazed up at her but I couldn't move. My body seemed trapped in my pain.

She sat down beside me. "You can't do this," she said. "You have too much to live for."

"No, I don't."

She put her arm around me. "Yes, you do. You have friends and people who love you. In the end that's all that counts. People love you because you're you. Not because you're good at something." She squeezed my shoulder. "And, Allie, lots of athletes play again after knee injuries. It's not like it used to be. I've done a bunch of research."

Parm always researched stuff for me. I covered my face with my hands. "What if I can't go to Duke next year? It's all I've ever dreamed of."

She pulled me close to her. "Just wait for the tests. Don't jump to conclusions."

"But . . . what will I do? Live in a closet because my room is gone?"

"Have you talked to your mom?" she asked softly.

I lifted my head and faced Parm. "She's getting married again."

Parm put her hand on my cheek and it felt warm and tender, but suddenly it made me recoil. I pushed away from her. "How could you? Don't touch me like that!"

With a shocked look on her face, Parm pulled her hand away and put it in her lap. "Allie, you're my friend," she said. "Nothing else."

Nothing else.

I bent over at the waist to pick up the pills and Parm grasped my wrists. "I would never jeopardize our friendship. It means way too much to me. I'm here for you. I want to help you."

What was I doing? Why was I acting so helpless? This was so not me. A dam burst inside me and I started crying. My body heaved and I could barely breathe. I couldn't stop the tears. Parm held me tight while I sobbed, patting my back.

"It's okay, Allie," she said in a soothing voice. "Keep crying. It will make you feel better."

Finally — I have no idea how much time later — I pulled back from her and wiped my nose with my hand.

She handed me a tissue. "You'll get through this," she said. "Crying is cathartic."

"My knee might be destroyed, Jonathon broke up with me, and I just treated you like crap when all you've been is good to me," I mumbled. "And I wanted to take pills. I'm acting stupid and like a jealous idiot. In the end, I'm just like my mother."

"We all make mistakes," Parm said. She paused for a second. "Hey to lighten you up, I just asked out that girl on your team, Jacquie, and she told me she had a girl-friend. I felt so stupid." Another pause. "We'll meet the right partners one day."

I tilted my head and stared at her. "Jacquie? Seriously?"

"Never mind," she said. "This isn't about me now. You need to think about you and your knee. That's your priority."

Parm stayed with me all night, sleeping on the floor beside my bed. I appreciated her company. She genuinely cared about me. I didn't want to be alone with myself. When I awoke in the morning, light shone through my curtains. I blinked. My eyes felt puffy and I was emotionally drained.

Parm was already awake and folding blankets. "How do you feel today?" she asked.

"Better," I said. I did feel better, and the new day made me realize how stupid I'd been. What had gotten into me? "I'm so sorry about last night." I hung my head. "I don't honestly think I would have done it."

"I hope not," said Parm.

I looked at her. "Please don't tell anyone."

"I won't," she said. "But I *am* worried."

"I'll be okay."

"I think you should see someone. A sports psychologist would help."

"Yeah, maybe I will."

"No maybe. You have to promise."

Parm was right. Last night had been dumb, a stupid moment, and I never wanted something like that to happen again. "Okay, I promise."

"Many injured athletes talk through their fears," stated Parm.

I sucked in a huge breath. "I know."

Fears. That was the word all right.

Coach Cathy called later in the afternoon to tell me the results were in and we had a doctor's appointment at four. At three thirty I was ready, dressed in sweats and a hoodie. When she pulled up in front of my house, I headed outside using my crutches.

As I hobbled to the car, I suddenly stopped and stared. Someone was in the passenger seat.

Mom.

When did she get here? How did she know? Coach Cathy must have called her. Or maybe Parm had. Or Carrie even.

Our eyes met. I watched as she opened the car door and stepped outside. "Allie," she said. Her black hair was cut short, and gone were her sleazy clothes and heavy eye makeup. For the first time since my dad left her, she looked respectable, like a mother. She reached out to hug me.

I was still in shock and didn't move. "Mom," I muttered, "what are you doing here?"

"I think you need me." She kept her arms open.

A lump formed in my throat. Then I moved into her arms, accepting the hug.

The hug lasted only a few seconds before I got in the back seat with my crutches. No one said a word all the way to the doctor's office. After waiting fifteen minutes in the waiting room, the three of us were ushered into a doctor's room. We sat like statues, until the doctor arrived. Coach Cathy stood up and shook his hand and so did my mother. I stayed seated, too filled with dread to struggle to my feet. He smiled at me and sat down in front of his computer.

He turned the computer screen so I could see an image of a knee. I held my breath.

"So, Allie," he said as he looked straight at me. He was hesitating. To me, that wasn't a good sign.

"Your knee has a few things going on with it." He pointed to the screen. "You have torn both your anterior cruciate ligament and your medial collateral ligament, and you have a severe meniscus tear." He pointed to the parts on the knee, but I wasn't really looking. His words had sunk into my brain and were bouncing around like hundreds of loose baseketballs.

From all my years in sport, I knew this was bad. Not only the two ligament tears, but the meniscus tear. Triple whammy. I wanted to ask questions but my mouth seemed to be sewn shut.

"What kind of rehab are we looking at?" Coach Cathy asked.

The doctor glanced at her before he turned again to me. "You'll need lots of physiotherapy, but because these tears are so severe, I'm not sure that physio alone will get you back to a hundred percent. Surgery is another option." He hesitated, and again I knew it wasn't a good sign. What else could he tell me?

At last he continued. "My biggest concern is that there seems to be some osteoarthritis showing in the knee. I would like to run more tests."

"Arthritis?" I finally spoke, my voice shaking. It didn't even sound like my voice.

"Arthritis," my mother echoed.

"You have very little cartilage holding this knee together." He turned to my mother. "Does anyone in your family have osteoarthritis?"

"Allie's paternal grandfather had it," my mother said quietly.

I'd never met my grandfather because he'd died before I was born, but in every old photo, he was in a wheelchair. Tears spilled down my cheeks. Was that going to be me? This was bad.

The doctor pretended I wasn't crying. "Medical science had changed a lot since then," he said. "Some of this injury could also be from continuous irritation from unrepaired torn meniscus or other injuries. That's why I'd like more tests."

I lowered my head and stared at my long fingers. I didn't want to look at the image of my knee anymore and I didn't want to look at this doctor's face. And I didn't want to hear how I had arthritis and ligament damage and a torn this and torn that. My mother put her hand on my shoulder and squeezed. Something about the warm familiar touch made me cry harder. The comfort she gave made me feel like a little girl again.

"If it is arthritis, what would that mean for Allie?" my mother asked the doctor.

"A full knee replacement might be an option," he replied.

Full knee replacement? I was only seventeen! My fingers scratched at my jeans. "What about my basketball?" I croaked.

"Well, if it is arthritis, I'm not sure you'll be able to play as an elite athlete." The doctor's voice was tender but firm. "You'll be able to lead a normal life, to walk, play golf, and do other recreational sports, but playing basketball at a college level might not be in your best interest."

Recreational? Had I heard him right? *Recreational?*

"Let's grab something to eat," said Coach Cathy once we were back in the car. She had picked my mom up at the airport just before my appointment, so Mom hadn't even checked into her hotel yet. And, yes, it had been Coach Cathy who'd made the call.

"I look awful," I said. And I wasn't hungry.

"You look like an athlete," said Coach Cathy.

"Yeah, one with a *bad* leg," I mumbled.

I agreed to go to a restaurant, and we managed to get a booth well away from other tables. We ordered a large Greek pizza.

As we waited for it to arrive, Coach Cathy started the conversation. "You'll need to start physio ASAP, Allie."

My mother twirled her water glass. "I really appreciate everything you've done for her."

I slouched in my seat. "I want to teach for you this

summer," I said to Coach Cathy, ignoring my mother. "I want to play at Duke next year. Like I'm supposed to."

"I know, Allie," said Coach Cathy. "But sometimes things happen that are beyond our control. I run the same camp every summer, so there will always be next year. Teaching and coaching will be something you can always do."

"You'll need a good physio and doctor in Halifax too," said my mother.

"You don't have money for that," I muttered.

"Mike knows a good sports physio and a doctor. He's been making some calls."

"How can you bring Mike into this?" I glared at her.

"Allie," said Coach Cathy, "help is good. Don't turn it away because you're angry at what life dealt you. Sometimes things happen for a reason. Have you ever thought about coaching? You'd be good. I started coaching after a severe back problem. I was supposed to play on the Olympic team but I couldn't."

I knew that about Coach Cathy, but I'd never even thought about how it must have been for her. She was my coach and just seemed to love what she was doing. "I'm sorry that happened to you," I said softly.

She slid out of her seat. "I'm going to the washroom before the pizza arrives." She patted my shoulder before she walked away.

Suddenly my mom and I were alone. I stared down at the tabletop. She leaned forward and reached for my hands, which she then gripped in her own. I refused to look up.

"Please let me help you," she said. "I know we've had a rough few years but I'm stronger now."

"How do I know that?" I didn't withdraw my hands or look up.

"You have to believe me."

Finally, I looked up and frowned. "You've been a horrible mother for years."

"You're right." Her eyes watered. "I relied on you too much," she said. "But you were so capable and strong. It was easy for me to let you do everything."

"I'm not strong anymore, okay?"

"Yes, you are, honey."

My throat constricted, and it was hard to breathe. After a few seconds I blurted out, "Are you really getting married again?"

I saw her flinch and I glared at her, waiting for her answer.

"Not for a while." She gently squeezed my hands. "I thought long and hard on the flight here. When I landed I immediately called Mike. Told him I think we're being impulsive." She gave a weak smile. "A bad habit of mine."

Thoughts flashed through my mind. Last night I'd also acted impulsively. And before that I'd acted needy and jealous with Jonathon. How many guys had I gone through last year? I glanced down at our hands and noticed how similar they were: long thin fingers, short stubby nails. Maybe the impulsiveness was in my genes. But if she could change, I could too.

"Right now," Mom continued, "you're my priority. Mike and I can wait. He said no rush." She stroked my fingers. "I want to be your mother again. We can get through this together. And I want you to have a chance to meet

Mike and get to know him before we do anything rash like get married."

I wanted to tell her that I didn't need her help and never had, but the words wouldn't come out because they weren't true. I did need her. And I did want her in my life.

Tears fell down my face. Mom tenderly wiped them away with a tissue she pulled from her purse. Then she got up and came over to slide into the seat beside me. She wrapped her arms around me and I let my head fall onto her shoulder. She stroked my hair and kissed the top of my head.

"We'll get through this, Allie," she said. "I love you so much."

"I love you too," I whispered.

CHAPTER FOURTEEN

My phone pinged as I flopped down on my bed. Coach Cathy had dropped me off before she took my mom to her hotel. Everyone at school had probably heard by now that I was done playing basketball for the year and would never play for Podium again. I couldn't finish my season with the teammates I loved playing with. We had plans for our last game, our last party, our goodbye. Oh sure, I could watch from the sidelines and cheer and still be part of the team in spirit, but that was not what I wanted to do. Coach Cathy asked if I could help her with practice and game plans. That was *some*thing, anyway.

The text was from Jonathon. He was at the front door. I texted him and told him the door was open. Could something positive come of today? He was such a good guy; I would take him back in heartbeat.

"Hey," he said, walking into my room. "I heard the news." I sat up and just the sight of him made my heart beat like crazy. He looked gorgeous in jeans and a blue hoodie, his hair still a little damp from showering. My body trembled and I wanted him to lie down beside me and hold me, and tell me everything was going to be okay between us.

He sat on the end of my bed. "I'm sorry," he said. "I heard it's not good."

"Nope. It's crappy." I paused for a moment before I said, "But I'll survive."

"How long will you have to rehab?" He looked stiff and awkward and his body language made my heart fall to my toes. This was not how I wanted him to look.

"No idea," I said. Then to keep the conversation going, I went on, "I'm going to finish my year at Podium. But other than that, everything is up in the air." I shrugged. "I might have to defer Duke for a year." That was my best-case scenario, but I wasn't going to whine to Jonathon.

"That's such a drag," he said. He didn't reach out to touch or comfort me, and he remained seated on the very end of the bed. "Maybe you could apply to some schools on the East Coast. I take it you'll head to Halifax in the summer to do rehab there."

"I guess so. Not what I want, though."

"I understand," he said.

An awkward silence hovered between us, and at last I blurted, "Are we done for good?" I swear the question just flew out of my mouth.

He scratched his denim-clad leg with his fingers, staring down at his thighs and not at me. "I think it's best," he said quietly.

"Why? Because of my knee?"

Immediately he looked up and gave me a puzzled look. "It has nothing to do with your knee. I like you a lot, Allie, but it's too much work to keep this relationship going when we fight all the time. Everything was great in the beginning — we laughed and had such a good time. Then things changed."

"You're blaming me?" I asked. In a way I *was* to blame. I had become this petty, jealous girlfriend. Me and my mom, we were quite thxe pair.

"I'm not blaming anyone," he said. "We just don't seem to work anymore. And next year would be even more difficult, trying to keep up a relationship long-distance. I . . . I don't want to start college that way." He paused and gave me a tentative smile. "I'd like to go to grad with you, though, that is, if you want to go with me."

"Let me think about it," I said, blinking back the tears.

Jonathon hadn't been gone for more than five minutes when my phone pinged again. This time it was Carrie — at the front door. I texted and told her it was open.

"Hey, girl, how're you doing?" she asked as soon as she came into my room. Then she scrunched up her face. "I'd say 'Chin up, buttercup,' but I'm not sure it's appropriate."

I quickly searched her face, and when I saw no hint that she knew about the pills, I breathed a sigh of relief. Parm, ever loyal, was true to her word.

"It's horrible," I said. "My knee is shot."

"Geez," she said. "I didn't want to hear that." She moved close to my bed. "Can you scrunch over with that two-ton-Tessie leg of yours? We need girl talk on the bed."

I shifted over to be closer to the wall and Carrie stretched out beside me, our bodies touching at the shoulder and leg. This is how we always talked things through.

"I probably can't go to Duke next year either," I said. "And I can't teach at the coach's summer camp. I might never play again." I stifled a sob. "This is so hard. What am I going to do next year?"

"Rehab, girl, and you'll get better. You can do this."

I glanced at her and she raised herself on one elbow and shook her finger at me. "You are the strongest chick I know and you are not a quitter. You hear me? Not a quitter."

"My mother is here," I said.

Her eyes widened. "She flew in?"

"Yeah."

"How'd that go?"

I paused a moment. "Good," I said. "I'm glad she's here." I realized I really meant it.

Carrie smiled and rested her head on my shoulder. "That's awesome, girl. If there's one thing I've learned from all my dumb mistakes, it's that you have to take help when you can get it."

"She admitted she screwed up," I said. "She's trying. So I'm going to try too. I'm going back to Halifax at the end of the school year. I guess I'll meet her new man if they haven't broken up by then."

"Summer's a long ways away." She did a little dance with her shoulders. "And we've got grad. Get that leg better so you can dance."

"Jonathon just broke up with me for good."

Carrie turned to look at me. "That sucks big-time. I'm so sorry." She wrinkled her nose. "But that's his loss, you know."

"I know."

"Maybe we're just not meant to have boyfriends," she said.

"He still wants me to go to grad with him." I rolled my eyes.

"Perfect." Carrie held up her thumb. "You go with your ex and I'll go with mine and we'll leave Podium in style."

I held up my hand and she slapped it.

"Oh my gawd!" I yelled. "Why is life so complicated?"

"Now, that's the Allie I know. Loud and feisty." Carrie grinned. "I've been waiting for you to get your Allie energy back. Okay, to answer your question. First we're teens. And that's a biggie all by its lonesome. But *we* have to add more. *We* throw competition in there because we have this crazy desire to be the best at something. So we train our butts off because we're so *driven,* not like most kids who just try to have fun."

"Crazy and obsessed," I added. And we were. All of us at Podium.

"Oh, and dump *high school* in there," said Carrie.

"And guys," I said. "Let's not forget about the guys."

"Yeah, they mess with our heads big-time until our brains become mush."

We started laughing and it felt good. I hadn't laughed in days.

But then I just stopped. Carrie eyed me. "I'm scared," I said. "We can laugh about how obsessed we are, but basketball is my life. What will I do without it?"

"Hey," she said softly. "I get ya. But right now, the verdict isn't in. You have to do that nasty rehab stuff. And I know you will. You'll do every exercise they give you and then some."

"I'm going to do everything in my power to get back on the court," I said.

"Just take it one day at a time. And know you've got lots of people who care about you. Look how your mom flew all the way out to make sure you were okay."

"Yeah." I nodded.

And it was at this moment that I knew I really *would* be okay. I had a team of family and friends. Yes, I would do everything I could to go to Duke the following year, but if it didn't work, I'd figure something out.

ACKNOWLEDGEMENTS

Where does the time go? It's so hard to believe that we are already on book six in the Podium Sports Academy series. When my wonderful editor, Carrie Gleason, and I first discussed the possibility of the series, the thought of book six seemed so far away. After all, I had yet to write the first book. What a pleasure it has been to work with Carrie for the first six books. She is an amazing editor who is positive when she provides her detailed editorial advice. I want to thank her for believing in me and this series. I also want to thank Kendra Martin, who works tirelessly behind the scenes to promote the series. She is genuinely happy when a good review comes in and does everything she can to get the book in the right hands. And, of course, I thank Jim Lorimer for continuing to publish such high-quality books. My final and biggest thanks is for you, my reader, for reading the sports stories I love to write.

ABOUT LORNA SCHULTZ NICHOLSON

Hoop Dreams is Lorna Schultz Nicholson's sixteenth novel and the sixth book in her Podium Sports Academy series. Lorna is also the author of seven non-fiction books and six picture books about hockey. Growing up in St. Catharines, Ontario, Lorna played volleyball, basketball, soccer, softball, and hockey, and was also a member of the Canadian National Rowing Team. She attended the University of Victoria, British Columbia, where she obtained a Bachelor of Science degree in Human Performance. From there Lorna worked in recreation centres, health clubs, and as a rowing coach until she turned her attention to writing. Today Lorna works as a full-time writer and does numerous school and library visits throughout the year to talk about her books. She divides her time between Calgary, Alberta, and Penticton, British Columbia, and lives with her husband, Hockey Canada President Bob Nicholson, and the three family dogs that keep her company while she writes.

"The series is designed to connect with teens by dramatically leading them through the possibilities their choices create and offering wholesome suggestions for successful outcomes. Author Lorna Schultz Nicholson achieves this without ever appearing to be preaching to the reader. Big Air *is highly recommended for any teens, and the series should be available in all middle years school libraries."* **Highly Recommended**
— Sherry Faller, *CM: Canadian Review of Materials*

"Lorna's books are a great read for kids and their parents. They really help teach the importance of having good values both in hockey and in life."
— Wayne Gretzky

"Podium Sports Academy gives readers a look into the life of a student-athlete. Through Lorna's books, we have an opportunity to develop an appreciation for the commitment and dedication necessary to maintain the delicate balance associated with being a teenager, athlete, and student."
— Ken Weipert, Principal, National Sport School, Calgary, AB

"These hi/lo books tackle difficult teen problems in an easy-to-read style."
— School Library Journal

BIG AIR

> Marc lived in Montreal. When did he get to Calgary? I had no idea he was coming west.
>
> My blood rushed through me — not in a good way, not how it did when I was flying through the air. I stood still, trying to slow my breathing. Marc's being here couldn't be good. Not good at all.
>
> *Control, Jax, control. He's your brother.*

Everything is going right for snowboarder Jax Barren. He's winning competitions and has a sponsor who keeps him in the newest boards and gear. But then Jax's troubled older brother, Marc, shows up at Podium Sports Academy, and Jax knows he's up to no good. Can Jax be a good brother to Marc, while at the same time avoid staying out of trouble so he can keep his sponsorship?

Buy the books online at www.lorimer.ca

DON'T MISS THIS BOOK!

FORWARD PASS

" I curled into a ball. *It was just a kiss.* Nothing sexual had happened.

Then a horrible thought hit me. What if the rest of the team found out? I didn't want this out now. Anyway, what if Caroline said I was making it up? Then I would never make it to the National Team. My hopes and dreams would die in an instant. "

Soccer player Parmita feels the right time to come out about her sexuality is after she's graduated from Podium Sports Academy. But when her coach makes a pass at her, she fears her secret will come out.

Buy the books online at www.lorimer.ca

VEGAS TRYOUT

 It's Vegas. And Vegas is all about how you look.

"You need to lose at least ten pounds." Coach snapped her book shut. "This had better change by next weigh-in. You're the shortest girl on this team and now you're the heaviest."

Lap after lap, I swam as hard as I could to get my frustration out.

Suck it up and swim, Carrie.

Synchro swimmer Carrie doesn't have the body shape that most athletes in her sport have, so when her coach takes her off the lift and puts her on a special diet, Carrie takes it too far.

Buy the books online at www.lorimer.ca

DON'T MISS THIS BOOK!

ONE CYCLE

 Short term is all I want. Maybe just one cycle. I need to get big quick."

"You're sure?" His eyes narrowed.

What was with this guy? Why did Ryan send me here? Did he buy off this guy? He was supposed to help me, not shoot me down.

"Positive.

Lacrosse player Nathan is smaller than the other players, but fast and a good team player. When he starts taking steroids, everything changes and more people than just him get hurt.

Buy the books online at www.lorimer.ca

DON'T MISS THIS BOOK!

ROOKIE

 I hated this.

I wanted the blindfold off and this to be over. I had a horrible feeling in my stomach. None of this was me. I just wanted to play hockey. *Stay tough,* I told myself. I tried to breathe.

"Let's execute," spat Ramsey.

Aaron Wong is away from home, a hockey-star-in-the-making at Podium Sports Academy. He's special enough to have earned his place at a top school for teen athletes — but not special enough to avoid the problems of growing up.

Buy the books online at www.lorimer.ca